# AMISH BACHELOR'S SECRET

SEVEN AMISH BACHELORS BOOK 7

SAMANTHA PRICE

ISBN 978-1-925689-47-1

# CHAPTER 1

BENJAMIN STOPPED at the front door of his parents' house and removed his dusty boots. Normally, he'd do that at the back door, but today he figured his *Mamm* wouldn't mind one transgression of her rigid rules. With his mother, everything had to be done just so. Looking down at his black socks, he was pleased they not only matched, but they had no holes. He'd tried to look his best for *Mamm* and had worn his Sunday suit for traveling home.

He placed his hand around the doorknob and twisted it. When it was open slightly, he called out, "I'm back!" He stepped inside, closed the door behind him, and breathed in the smell of home-baked bread mixed with a hint of roast. He was certain the air also held a whiff of the cream that went into the middle of the whoopie pies. *Ah, whoopie pies.* He'd missed his mother's cooking.

The sight of his mother's smiling face and chubby cheeks as she ran toward him filled him with happiness. Ivy rushed to hug her son and he stepped forward, lifted her up, and swung her in a circle.

She chuckled as she scolded him. "Oh, goodness, let me go." He placed her down on the floor. "Now, Benjamin, let me look at you. Off with the hat." Once he removed it, she smoothed down his dark hair, and then her gaze traveled down him, right down to his socks. Ivy placed her hands on his arms and held him out at arm's length. "You're tanned, and you look so much older."

*"Denke* ... I think. More handsome too?"

Ivy giggled at her son's cheekiness and then with the back of her hand she touched his cheek. "You've still got soft baby skin."

*"Jah,"* he joked, "it's the special oil, and the same one I use on the buggy leathers." When she didn't stop touching his cheeks, he removed her hand. "Stop it, *Mamm.* I'm a grown man." He replaced his hat hoping that would stop her fussing.

She chuckled. "You'll always be my *topple."* She moved in and hugged him tight with both arms around his waist.

Benjamin rolled his eyes. "Don't carry on like this if I ever bring a girl here."

"Come into the kitchen. You could've come home at least once to see us. Why couldn't you have done that?"

"I dunno; it just wasn't convenient at the time. I wrote to you, though."

He placed his backpack down just inside the doorway as he followed her into the kitchen. He knew it was his parents' greatest desire he come home with a wife after traveling for five years, but he saw no point in marrying for the sake of marrying. He'd thought he'd been in love many times, but that only lasted a while before the feeling left as quickly as it had arrived. He was relieved to be home. It was hard to relax in someone else's house, and it seemed that every few weeks he'd had to adjust to new circumstances.

As she busied herself fixing him a snack, she said, "*Dat* will be home soon, and then we have dinner tomorrow night with the whole family. I was going to have it tonight, but I thought you'd be tired."

He sat down at the kitchen table. "Great. I'm looking forward to it. And you're right, I am exhausted. Right now, I need to sleep." He took off his hat once more and place it on the table, running the other hand through his nearly shoulder-length hair. "I can't wait to see Taylor and Timothy's new *boppli.* Aaron, isn't it?" Benjamin was closest with his brother, Timothy, being also closest to him in age.

"*Jah,* and you haven't seen their second one yet either."

"I know, *Mamm.* I know exactly how many nieces and nephews I've got. Isaac, the favored and firstborn, is the forerunner with four. Everyone else has two except for Taylor and Timothy who are hot on Isaac and Hazel's heels with three. I am the only one with zero."

"And whose fault is that?" She placed a plate of chocolate chip cookies on the table. "And, you're wrong. Mary Lou and Jacob have three now Jimmy's come along."

He scratched his neck. "Oh, didn't I say that?"

"*Nee*. You were wrong just like you're wrong about wasting time finding a *fraa*." She shook a finger at him. "You're not so clever. Not as clever as you think."

Benjamin's jaw dropped open. "I've been looking for someone, *Mamm,* and I am looking forward to your cooking, but I've only just eaten. I didn't know if you'd have anything for me or not."

"I'll make you a nice hot cup of tea before bedtime. You've certainly been active with women enough from what I've heard. I've learned you've had about five girlfriends since you've been gone. Wouldn't one of them have made you a suitable *fraa?*"

He glanced at his hat sitting where he'd absent-mindedly placed it on the table. It was a little surprising he hadn't been reprimanded for not hanging it on one of the hooks behind the front door. She wasn't looking now, as she'd just turned the stove on and was filling the teapot up with tealeaves. He didn't like hot tea, but she'd forgotten that.

He'd suffer through it just this once. "Possibly,

*Mamm,* but I'm looking for more than just someone suitable. I'm looking for the best there ever was." He chuckled when he saw the horrified look on his mother's face. He loved to tease her. Part of what he said was true. He only wanted to marry when he was truly in love, and not be forced into marriage because it was expected. Besides, his mother and father had enough *grosskinner.* His brothers had all done their duties and married appropriately, except maybe for Timothy, but things had gone well for him since he married Taylor.

"Don't expect too much. Girls are only human and everyone has faults." She replaced the lid of the china teapot and stepped even closer, crouched lower, and wagged a finger in his face. "Benjamin, you need to lower your standards."

"Hmm, is that what *Dat* did when he married you?"

She straightened up. "Benjamin! What a dreadful thing to say."

He rubbed the side of his nose. "Well, it does make my point, doesn't it? Isn't lowering one's standards a bad thing? I'm happy with my standards just how they are."

"You're impossible. Just impossible." She turned away and opened the cups' and saucers' cupboard.

"So, are you glad I'm back?"

She stared at him until her face broke into a smile. "I'm glad you're back." She closed the cupboard and hurried toward him and wrapped her arms around her son's shoulders. She hugged him tight and Benjamin's body shook with laughter.

"Am I ever going to get that tea, or what?"

"I haven't ever been separated from any of you boys for so long."

He remained silent as she finished making the tea. It had been his parents' idea for him to go away, didn't she remember? He was only in his mid-twenties and he didn't see why everyone was in a rush for him to be married. He'd had an eventful time away and now he had to make his mother understand there was more to life than finding him a *fraa.* He knew, at some of the places he'd been, *Mamm* had friends who'd written to her to tell her what he'd been doing. That's how she'd found out about the girls he'd dated.

He had to show her he was a man now and make it clear she and *Dat* couldn't push him around. He cleared his throat. "At some of the places I was, I volunteered as a firefighter, and I loved it. I'm going to do the same here."

"That's *gut.*" She proceeded to make the tea. He'd expected more of a reaction, like her telling him it was too dangerous. "Our *familye* has always done community service. I'm happy to see you're carrying that on."

Maybe she didn't get how hazardous it could be. "I know the boys help out people in the community, like clearing out rubbish, chopping firewood and the likes, but firefighting can be ... well there is the possibility I'll have to attend a dangerous fire." If anything bad happened to him, he didn't want it to come as a shock. She had to know there was danger, to be prepared.

"You've done the training?" she asked.

*"Jah,* of course."

"Then you'll know what to do."

*Hmmm, maybe things have changed around here,* he thought. She sat down in front of him with two cups and the teapot. "So, what's new, *Mamm?* What's changed since I've been gone?"

For the next half hour, he got up to speed on what his brothers and their wives had done. She finished with, "And naturally, you'll go back to work with your *vadder."*

It wasn't a question. It seemed more of a command. He wasn't sure if he wanted to work in the family business again. "I thought he'd retired."

"Semi-retired."

"Ah, semi-retired, as in he still goes to work every day and interferes with Isaac's management?"

Her mouth fell open. "I wouldn't say so."

"Okay, nothing has changed at work. What's new with you?"

"I think people are finally forgetting about what happened with Timothy and Taylor. Taylor has proved herself to be a solid member of the community."

"It's sad people have to prove themselves. Why can't people just be what they are and others stop judging them?"

His mother's mouth tightened and tiny lines appeared around it. "They don't."

"They do. You just said it."

She leaned over. "It was shameful how they got married just a day before their first *boppli* arrived."

"I see what you mean. But I thought that was much better than them getting married after, or not at all, with a baby in the mix." He picked up the teapot and poured them each a cup. When he brought the teacup to his lips and had a sip, he said, "I wish people wouldn't be so judgemental sometimes, that's all."

"Let's not ruin this reunion with your liberal thinking, Benjamin. You seem to have gathered a few strange ideas with your travels."

He tried to keep the smile from his face. "Let's talk of something else then. When will *Dat* be home?"

Her gaze traveled to the clock by the stove. "In another hour."

"Hmm, I'll be asleep by then. I'll have to see him in the morning."

"*Jah,* you'll have to talk to him about work."

He took another sip of tea. "I'll talk to Isaac about it if that's what I decide I want. He's the one in charge. He was when I left, since *Dat* handed him the reins, so to speak." His mother moved uncomfortably in her chair, and Benjamin didn't envy Isaac one little bit for being in charge, especially because every day he had their father watching over his shoulder and judging and questioning everything he did. In a small way,

Benjamin felt like he'd be going backward in life if he returned to what he'd been doing before he left. He wanted to go forward with his life rather than backward. He'd learned many new skills on his travels, and now there were so many other things he could do.

One thing Benjamin knew, he was going to sign up to be a volunteer firefighter the very next day.

# CHAPTER 2

"I'M DESTINED FOR HEARTACHE, Mary Lou."

Mary Lou sat nursing Jimmy, her six-month-old baby, while her glum-faced cousin, Magnolia, sat on the couch opposite her complaining about one thing after another. "You can't say that, Magnolia. No one is destined for heartache. If things haven't been working for you romantically, you just have to change what you've been doing."

"I don't see how it will make a difference. I was dating Rodrick for two years, and he never proposed. I thought I'd have better luck with David and after six months he hadn't proposed. I said to David, *marry me or we're through.* I wrote it in a note to him and at the end of the word *through,* I used one of those marks with the dots at the bottom. What are they called again?"

"Exclamation marks?"

"That's right. I put three of them after the word, *through.*"

Mary Lou pulled a face. "You wrote him a note saying, *marry me or else,* and you used three exclamation marks? That would hardly make him feel loving toward you and want to propose to you, or marry you. What were you thinking?"

"Mary Lou, you're not listening again. I didn't say, *or else.*" Magnolia screwed up her face.

"Can't you see that was the tone of your note? And why write a note at all? Why couldn't you have just talked to him face-to-face?" When Magnolia wiped away a tear Mary Lou adjusted the volume of her voice, adopting a softer expression and telling herself to be more sympathetic. "So, what happened?"

"Well, that's when I got your letter. And I thought if I came here it would make him miss me. But when he found out I was coming here, he thought I was looking for someone else. He threw his hands up in the air, and said, *let's just forget the whole thing.* Then he walked away."

"That's dreadful. What happened then?"

"I followed him and I said, *fine if you want to forget it as easy as that, that's good because I'll forget it, I'll forget everything, and I'll forget you like I never knew you.*"

Mary Lou grimaced. "Is that all?"

"I might have said, *I hate you.*"

"Magnolia!"

Magnolia shrugged. "I do. He didn't love me at all. He couldn't have if he just walked away."

Mary Lou wondered if anyone at all would be able to get along with her cousin. She no longer had the puffy cheeks and the full figure of the Magnolia from five years ago. She'd slimmed down and even looked taller. Magnolia's appearance had improved, but the sour look on her face and her sharp-edged personality needed work if she ever wanted to find a healthy relationship. "If I've learned one thing since I've been married, it's communication. You really need to talk about things to know what the other one is thinking. Men just don't think the same as women. I'm not certain why that is, but they don't."

Magnolia sniffed and nodded. "It might have been my fault. I think I got too upset with him, but I was through with the waiting. Now, I'm just so lonely, and I feel so unlovable."

"I'm so sorry to hear it." Her baby finished feeding, and Mary Lou did up the front of her dress and placed him over her shoulder to burp.

"First, I'd been strung along, and then I thought things would be different with my second romance, but it wasn't."

Mary Lou nodded. She could relate to someone stringing her along. Isaac had courted her for two years and then ended things with her to marry Hazel. It was heart breaking at the time, but now she was grateful.

She was very much in love with Jacob and together they had been blessed with three beautiful children.

Magnolia's gaze dropped to the quilt beside Mary Lou, who sewed in her spare time. It was already a thing of beauty, sprawled across the couch next to her. "Where are your other *kinner?*"

"At Ivy's."

"I can't wait to meet them. I've been away for so long, and I can't believe you've got *kinner* already."

"Adam is three and Lucinda is two. I'm telling you, they're so cute. I'm not saying it just because they're mine."

"I'll see for myself soon," Magnolia said.

"Adam looks after Lucinda and passes her toys, and when they walk hand-in-hand it just melts my heart. I've been so blessed."

"Good for you, but I'm here because of the promise you made. I'm not here to listen to you boast about your *wunderbaar kinner.*"

If Magnolia hadn't been so distraught, Mary Lou would've given her a piece of her mind, but the timing was wrong. "Err, about finding you a man?"

Magnolia nodded.

"You shouldn't have left it so long before you came back. I have been keeping an eye open for somebody. Well, I had been, up until I thought you had found somebody."

"I only wrote that in my letters because I thought I

had found somebody too." She shook her head and looked at the floor. "Nothing works out for me."

"I know it might seem like it now, but things will change one day soon. I was sad and angry when Isaac dumped me, and then not too long after I married Jacob."

"Stop!" Magnolia put her hand up. "That's what everybody keeps telling me, but when will it happen for me? And don't tell me to be patient. I'm through with being patient. I've been patient long enough."

Mary Lou giggled.

Magnolia pouted. "What's so funny?"

"You said you're through with being patient."

"I am." Magnolia's eyebrows rose.

"I know. It struck me as funny, that's all." Jimmy let out a loud burp, which made both girls giggle.

Magnolia stretched her hands out. "Can I hold him now?"

"*Jam*, of course."

Once Magnolia had the baby securely in her arms she gently rocked him. "I just love *babies*. Anyway, last time I was here there were two widowers. I wasn't interested in them at the time, but I think I am now."

"You'd consider marrying a widower now?"

"I guess so. I'm ready to look after someone else's *kinner* especially if they're as cute as this." She smiled as she stared at Jimmy. "He's closing his eyes."

"He's due for a sleep. That's a shame, what you said about the widowers because they're both married now.

They both married around a year and a half ago, within weeks of one another. Both of the wives are expecting now, too."

Magnolia stood up, passed the baby back to Mary Lou and Mary Lou looked on as Magnolia's cheeks turn beet red. Then Mary Lou gasped with horror when Magnolia kicked the stone frame of the fireplace, hard, with her booted foot. Mary Lou wondered if Magnolia had hurt herself.

Then slowly, Magnolia looked at Mary Lou, returned to the couch, and sat back down. "I'm sorry about that. I'm just feeling so wretched. Will I ever know the love of a good man, one who wants me and me alone?"

Mary Lou was tempted to say no because then Magnolia would leave, but she couldn't be so cruel. Besides, her heart was racing from the scene she'd just witnessed and she didn't want to further upset her cousin. The only solution was to find her a man and fast. "There is one man I know of."

"I'll take him," Magnolia said.

Mary Lou smiled. "I haven't even told you about him."

Magnolia rushed to sit on the floor beside Mary Lou, and she looked up at her. "So get on with it! Tell me all about him."

"His name is Zachariah Reid. Everyone calls him Zach."

*"Yah?* Go on. I like his name."

"Oh, I forgot, he's just left." Mary Lou felt dreadful for getting her cousin's hopes up. "I'm sorry."

"What do you mean, he's just left? Left for where?"

Mary Lou sighed and patted her baby hoping he'd go to sleep. "He was living here with his *schweschder,* Pattie, but then he left to get a job doing something or other with horses. Anyway, their parents died years ago and now Pattie is living on her own in the *haus.* I'm sorry, I shouldn't have mentioned him. I don't know what's wrong with me."

"Where's he gone?" Magnolia asked, sitting back on the chair.

"Somewhere in Chester County. Unionville, I think I heard."

"Hmm, that's not too far away. He'd have to come back to visit his *schweschder,* wouldn't he?"

"He's only just left a few weeks ago. It would need to be some kind of emergency for him to come back now."

"Tell me about him anyway. How old is he and what does he look like?"

"He's handsome, he's a little younger than you, but not by much. He's tanned from working outdoors, and he's got sandy-colored hair and green eyes."

"Wouldn't he have been here last time I was here?"

"I can't really say. I think so."

Magnolia shook her head. "I don't remember him. Has he had a girlfriend?"

"I can't recall. Possibly." Mary Lou changed the

subject. It was pointless talking about Zach. "The Fullers are having a family dinner tomorrow night. Would you like to go?"

"*Jah, denke,* I'll go."

"Benjamin's back."

"Back from where?"

"Traveling around here and there. He's a restless kind of person I think. Now he's got the traveling bug out of his system, he might be ready to settle down."

"*Nee,* not with me. We don't get along."

"*Ach nee,* I don't think the two of you would be a *gut* match. I meant for someone else. I do like matchmaking." A giggle escaped Mary Lou's lips.

"I liked him a little bit once, but then I grew out of it. It'll be nice to see him. So, how long has he been gone?"

"He left not long after Taylor and Timothy got married."

"Ah, so just after my last visit."

"Probably around that time, *jah.* Has it been so long since you've been here?"

"*Jah.* I haven't seen any of your *kinner,* remember? You haven't been to visit me, either."

# CHAPTER 3

BENJAMIN WAS OVERWHELMED with all the new nieces and nephews. They were all in the narrow age range of babies to toddlers, with Abe being the eldest. Taylor and Timothy's third child, Aaron, was the youngest. In a few years, the children would be a whole lot of fun to play with once they could run and kick a ball around.

His brothers and their wives hadn't changed in appearance at all, but he was a little distressed his father had aged considerably.

Once they were in the middle of their dinner, the conversation came around to Benjamin, as he knew it would. They'd all want to know exactly what he'd been doing. He'd have to be sure to keep his story straight.

"*MAMM* SAYS you're going to volunteer as a firefighter," Isaac said to Benjamin.

"*Jah,* I signed up today."

Magnolia, who was sitting beside him, said, "Isn't it dangerous?"

He'd been a little surprised to see Magnolia come with Jacob and Mary Lou. No one had warned him she'd be at the dinner. "It can be."

"Are you called out to *haus* fires?" Hazel asked.

"*Jah,* all kinds of fires. The worst are those deliberately set by arsonists." He couldn't believe people would deliberately light fires to watch lives be ruined and endangered, not to mention wildlife, businesses, and crops.

"What's that?" Magnolia asked.

Benjamin faced her. "Some people deliberately start fires, and they're called arsonists."

"That's awful. Why would anyone do that?" his *mudder* asked.

"All sorts of reasons. To collect insurance money, for revenge, or simply to gain excitement by watching the flames."

Mr. Fuller grunted. "Takes all sorts to make the world."

"There's so much evil out there," Adeline said.

"How do these people start the fires mostly?" Magnolia asked.

"Kerosene or some other kind of accelerant."

"What other sorts of accelerants?"

"Gasoline, turps ..."

"Can we please talk about something happier?" Adeline asked.

Benjamin chuckled. *"Jah,* I'm sorry, everyone. I get carried away sometimes."

"I hope you stay safe, Benjamin," Hazel said.

"As do we all," Lucy added.

Benjamin smiled and nodded to his sisters-in-law. All his brothers had married nice girls and he wanted someone like that for himself, if God willed it. His extended family was rapidly multiplying and their long table was now crowded with barely any elbow room. Even the children's dinner table would soon have to be replaced with one bigger, or they'd need a second one. The adults' table would only need to fit one more when he married, but the children could multiply up to three or four times as many. Just as well his parents had a large home.

When the meal was over, his mother cleared the table and, with the help of a couple of her daughters-in-law, washed up. Meanwhile, everyone else went to the living room and waited to be served an after-dinner coffee.

To Benjamin's annoyance, as soon as Isaac stood to put more logs on the fire, Magnolia sat down next to him, taking Isaac's place. "So, you've just come back here and so have I. I've been gone for nearly the same amount of time." Her head tilted back and she looked at the ceiling. "I think I left before you, and we've both been gone a long time." Now she was cackling while staring at him.

"And, what have you been doing, Magnolia?"

"Nothing much at all. Then, Mary Lou said she'd like to see me again. I mean, she must've written me half a dozen letters over the years begging me to come stay with her, until I finally felt sorry for her and agreed."

Benjamin glanced over at Mary Lou holding her baby. She was talking to Adeline and wasn't listening to their conversation. "And, why did you feel sorry for her?"

"She doesn't have a lot of family around."

"She's got us, and her folks too."

Isaac turned around and saw his seat was taken, and then he walked across to an open seat on the other side of the room. Magnolia acted completely unaware of having taken his seat.

"*Jah,* but Mary Lou and I have a special connection."

*Not too special,* Benjamin thought, *if you haven't visited for so long a time.*

"Are you back working with your brothers, Benjamin?"

"*Nee,* not yet."

"When do you start?"

He looked around, hoping no one would hear him. He hadn't yet shared his thoughts with any of his brothers. "I'm not sure what I'm going to be doing yet."

"What?" She shrieked so loudly everyone stopped

talking and looked at them. She calmed herself before continuing. "How can you not be sure? Are you trying to find yourself, or something?"

When the others started talking again, he said, "I've got other ideas I might want to explore."

"Like what?"

"Many things."

"Like firefighting?"

"I'm doing it. I've already signed on as a volunteer."

"How exciting. I wonder if they take women."

"They do, at least the *Englisch* crews include women, but I don't know if the bishop would like you volunteering. You have to wear a fire-resistant suit—pants. They're like overalls."

"Oh, well. Is the training hard?"

He nodded. "It sure is." He hadn't seen his family for so long, and now Magnolia was talking so much he couldn't talk with anyone else. "It's rewarding, though."

*"Jah,* I know many Amish men do it where I come from."

"Magnolia, would you like to hold Jimmy while I see if *Mamm* and the others need help?"

*"Jah."* Magnolia jumped up and walked over to Mary Lou.

Benjamin was freed up to play with his young nieces and nephews, who were sitting on a blanket littered with wooden toys and being watched over by Catherine and Adeline.

When the coffee arrived, Timothy told Catherine

and Adeline that Benjamin and he would watch the *kinner.* Timothy had Aaron, his youngest, in his arms, and then Benjamin asked if he could hold him.

"I've been waiting to talk with you, Timothy" Benjamin said. "It's strange to see you married and with three *kinner.*"

"I know. My whole life has changed, and I owe it in part to you."

Benjamin chuckled. "To me?"

*"Jah,* it was your idea to build us a *haus,* and you gave us the land you'd chosen."

"I know, and then you take the name, "Aaron." I was always going to call one of mine Aaron if I ever got married." When he saw the distressed look on Timothy's face, he said, "It was *Dat's* and *Mamm's* land. It was never mine. It was just a hazy idea in the back of my mind. And I'll use Aaron as a middle name, so don't feel bad."

Timothy laughed. "I'm glad you're back. You'll liven us all up."

Timothy looked over at the family, and Benjamin followed his gaze to Taylor. "She looks happy," Benjamin said.

*"Jah,* it took a while to train her."

Benjamin nodded knowing Timothy was now having fun with him. Taylor was a modern woman, and not one to be bossed about by a man. "You'd better not let her hear you say that."

Timothy nodded. "We're a good team, and believe it or not, she does listen to me and takes my advice."

"Glad to hear it."

"I thank *Gott* every day for my *familye.* Taylor and I nearly didn't marry. It was a close call." He rubbed his chin and then grabbed one of the toddlers who was trying to get off the rug. He sat him back down while handing him a toy.

"Ah, I can see you're well practiced with children," Benjamin said.

"*Jah,* I have to be." Timothy moved closer. "I think *Mamm's* out to find you a *fraa,* just between us."

Benjamin pulled a face. "I already knew it would happen soon enough. It mightn't be so bad. She might find me someone I like."

"I hope so, for your sake."

IT HAD BEEN nice to see everyone, but it was a relief when they'd all left because by then all Benjamin wanted to do was sleep. Isaac hadn't mentioned him returning to work, and whether it was because he was trying to give him space or because there was no job for him, he didn't know.

# CHAPTER 4

THROUGHOUT THE NIGHT when he was sleeping, Benjamin had become practiced at keeping an ear out for the phone. He was only half asleep on Monday night when he heard the family's phone ringing from the barn. At that time of night, it had to mean an emergency. He pulled on the pants he'd learned to drape over the footboard of the bed, stepped into the shoes he kept right beside his bed, grabbed his flashlight and raced out of the house to the phone.

He grabbed hold of the phone's receiver, pleased the caller hadn't hung up. *"Jah?"*

"There's a fire in progress at 66 Huckleberry Lane."

"I'm ready." He hung up, and ran into the house to get into the rest of his clothes before he ran to the bottom of the drive to wait for the fire truck.

As he waited, he tried to figure out who lived at 66 Huckleberry Lane. It was familiar to him. Then he realized it was the Reids' house. He'd gotten a letter soon after he left home telling him Mr. and Mrs. Reid had died within weeks of one another, leaving their son and daughter, Zachariah and Pattie. He sent up a prayer for God to protect them both, Pattie, and his friend, Zach.

Soon, he saw the flashing lights of the truck and got ready to jump in when it slowed to collect him. Once he was in the truck, one of the guys threw him a safety suit. He pulled it on and, in no time, they were at the Reid's house. When he and the rest of the men jumped down from the truck, orders were barked out at them and they all quickly followed their instructions. The fire was already well-established and flames billowed out through the roof of the small home.

As Benjamin helped hold one of the hoses aimed at the house, they were told no one was inside. He couldn't help but notice a small teenage girl by the ambulance being fussed over by a few EMTs. It had to be young Pattie Reid.

When the fire was out and what was left of the house was smouldering, he made his way over to Pattie, who was sitting still and wrapped in a blanket. "Are you okay?"

She looked up at him. "Benjamin?" He gave a quick nod. "My *haus* is gone. My *bruder* is away, and I have nowhere to live."

He sat down beside her. He was relieved to know for sure there'd been no casualties. "Where's Zach?"

"He left a few months ago for Unionville to get work, and now I live here alone"

"Are you hurt?"

She shook her head and looked down. "I'm okay. I'm completely unharmed. It was late, but I hadn't gone to bed yet. Then I heard something and went outside to check, to make sure there wasn't a problem with the horses or anything. When I looked back at the house, the whole side of it was on fire. I ran to the shanty and called 911."

"Smart. It's good you didn't try to go back inside. Stay with my parents. They have a huge *haus* and now it's just me and them."

She shook her head.

"You must. Do you have anywhere else to stay? Relatives?"

*"Nee.* But I could ..." Her attention was taken by a police car pulling up. Two officers got out and someone pointed out Pattie to them.

"Looks like they need to ask you a few questions. I'll hang around." Benjamin stayed back a distance, but close enough so he could hear what was said. They asked many questions, and then more questions, and when they asked where she'd be staying, he stepped forward and gave them his address.

"And what is your relationship to Miss Reid?" the taller of the officers asked him.

"We're in the same community, and she's a close friend of the family."

They took down Benjamin's address and phone number.

IT WAS daybreak when the fire truck gave Benjamin and Pattie a ride back to his house.

His mother must've seen them from the window because she came hurrying out of the house. Pattie was still visibly shaken, and wrapped in a fire department blanket.

"What's happened?"

"Pattie's *haus* has burned down and I said she could stay with us."

Benjamin was edged out of the way and his mother placed her arm around Pattie. "Oh, you poor mite. Of course you can. Come with me. I've got a bedroom made up. It was Timothy's old room. Have you eaten? *Nee,* you wouldn't have. I'll fix you something."

"First, I need to call my *bruder,* if that's okay." Pattie's voice was small and weak.

*"Jah,* certainly. Go with her, Benjamin, and show her where the phone is."

Once Pattie was back inside after making her call, and busy eating her way through a stack of pancakes, Mrs. Fuller pulled Benjamin aside. "What happened?"

"I'm not sure. They think it was arson. They found two cans of a commonly used accelerant by the back of the *haus.*"

Mrs. Fuller's mouth fell open. "That's awful. Who would want to do that?"

"I don't know. Sometimes those types of people do it for entertainment, like I was saying at dinner the other night."

"Shame on them."

He scratched the side of his face. "Her *bruder's* coming back as soon as he can."

"Then he must stay with us, too. He'll have nowhere else to go."

Benjamin nodded. "I kind of already said he could. It makes sense the two of them should be together."

*"Gut."* Lines marred his mother's worried forehead. "I'll make up a room for him."

When his mother hurried away, Benjamin sat down at the table with Pattie. She looked up at him with big brown eyes. *"Denke,* Benjamin."

"I've done nothing."

"You brought me here, and you worked on saving ... on trying to save my *haus."*

"You already thanked us all for that."

"I'm giving you special thanks."

He leaned forward, "You might be cursing me in a couple of days."

She giggled. "I don't think so."

"You see, *Mamm* might seem quiet now, but just you wait. She can turn into a monster."

She laughed. "You always were funny."

He looked down at the pancakes and shook his

head. "I warned you."

"Have one." She pushed the plate toward him.

*"Denke,* I will. I've missed *Mamm's* cooking."

"Where have you been? I didn't think of it until now, but I haven't seen you 'round lately."

He was just about to bite into his pancake, but he stopped to answer. "I've been gone for years. You didn't notice?"

She shook her head. "Maybe I got you mixed up with your other brothers. There are so many of you."

"I don't see how. I'm the more handsome one. Most handsome, I should say."

"Um, you all look pretty similar to me. Wait, now I know who you are. You're the one who was dating my cousin, Georgia. She's a cousin on my *vadder's* side."

He winced when he heard the name. She'd been one of the girls he'd dated over the past couple of years. Things didn't end well between them. She was trying to hurry him along to get married.

"And then six months later, you dated a cousin on my *mudder's* side, from Reading."

He'd dated two or three girls from there. "Can you be more specific?"

She nodded her head at him. "Marlene."

"Ah, Marlene Hostetler." He only vaguely remembered her, and he'd thought her name was Marjorie. "Hmm, so I dated two of your cousins?"

*"Jah."*

He had to change the subject, and right now. "How

old are you now, Pattie?"

"I'm seventeen."

Seventeen-year-old Amish girls had one thing on their minds and that was finding suitable husbands, but she didn't seem to be attracted to him at all. He studied her as she sat in silence eating the last pancake. She was paying far more attention to the food than she was to him. Then he thought again; her house had just burned down, so she was understandably distracted. Her big brown eyes suited her heart-shaped face perfectly. With her full lips and sandy-colored hair, she'd be a real beauty in a few years when she blossomed. Right now, she looked more like a kid, especially with the light smattering of freckles across her cheeks and nose.

She looked up at him. "Was I chewing too loud?"

The question caught him off guard and he chuckled. *"Nee."*

"My *bruder* always says I eat too noisily."

"Not at all. I didn't even hear you."

"Good." She ate some more. "That's a relief. Your *Mamm* is very kind. She doesn't have to have me here. I can always stay with the Wests. They kind of keep an eye out for me."

*"Nee,* you'll stay here. Your *bruder* is coming soon and he'll be staying here too, as soon as he gets back."

She sighed. *"Denke.* I hope he doesn't blame me for the fire."

"Of course he won't."

"How do you know?'

"You heard the police. They think it was started deliberately."

"Who by?"

"Dunno." He shrugged his shoulders. "The community will rebuild your *haus.* You don't have to worry about a thing."

"I was thinking of moving somewhere anyway. This could be a sign from *Gott* this place is not for me."

He suddenly felt protective of her and didn't want her to move anywhere. "That's nonsense."

"Is it?"

"*Jah.* Your parents were born here and so were you."

She shrugged her shoulders. "And my grandparents, and their parents, too. They built the *haus.* My great grandfather, I mean. Now, everything's in ashes and my parents are dead. Maybe I should move away with Zach."

"Don't do anything in haste. You might come to regret it. Let the community rebuild your house and then, if you decide to move on, you and Zach will have something to sell. That will be money for you to start a new life somewhere else."

She breathed out a long slow breath. "It feels weird. Everything I owned was in my home. Everything I loved, the things that reminded me of my parents and of their parents." She looked down at her clothes. "This is all I own now."

"No problem with the clothes part. I've got plenty of *schweschders*-in-law and they'll have spare dresses and *kapps.* One of them, Mary Lou, is an excellent sewer, so I'm told."

Her eyes twinkled as though he was telling another of his stories. "Who told you she was a good sewer?"

"Mmm, she did, I think." Pattie managed a wobbly smile, and Benjamin knew she was upset. "I know it must be devastating for you right now. I've talked to many people who've lost everything in a fire. One man said he felt like someone ripped out the ground from underneath him."

"That's exactly what it feels like. I didn't really have much. I guess that made what I did have even more special. I kind of feel like how I felt when *Dat* died. *Mamm* died first, but I still had *Dat.* Then he died. I feel orphaned all over again."

He couldn't imagine how that would feel at her young age. He didn't know much about her circumstances, only that her *bruder* had recently moved and her parents had died a few years ago. "I'm so sorry, this must be just awful." How did she support herself? "Do you have a job you need to go to today?"

"I work at a bed and breakfast, cleaning and doing odd jobs, but I only work Wednesday through Saturday. Do you think your folks would let me have my two horses over here?"

*"Jah.* They surely will. There's plenty of space for them. I'll fetch them later today for you."

*"Denke.* I'll go with you."

"Do you have any other livestock?"

"*Nee.* I gave the chickens away when Zach was leaving. I don't really cook enough to use all the eggs and there was no point keeping them. My dog died last year and I couldn't bear to replace him. So, it was just me, Chester, and Winnie."

"The horses?"

"*Jah.*"

Mrs. Fuller bustled back into the room. "I've got a room ready for you and one ready for your *bruder.*"

"*Denke,* Mrs. Fuller. I'm so grateful."

"And, the bathroom's at the end of the hallway, when you want to wash up."

Pattie looked down at her clothes. "I'll guess these clothes will need washing."

"*Mamm,* Pattie and I will go back to fetch her horses and while we're gone, do you think you could find her some clothes?"

"*Jah,* I'll go to Hazel's *haus.* Mine would fall off you. Hazel should have some spares, and Mary Lou's always showing up in newly sewn clothes. She'll have plenty too."

"That's very kind."

"Do you want me to hitch the buggy for you, *Mamm?* I'll take the wagon to get the horses, so they can be tethered alongside."

"*Jah,* hitch the buggy, please, and stay away from the busy roads with those horses. How many of them are there?"

"There are only two," Pattie said.

## CHAPTER 5

WHEN BENJAMIN APPROACHED Pattie's house, he regretted having brought her along. The remains of the house were black, and there were only charred bits of the frame left standing along with the stone foundations.

"My great *grossdaddi* built the *haus,* and now it's gone. I can't help feeling responsible."

"You're not. You can't think like that. You were lucky to get out of there. You could've been killed."

Pattie nodded. "I know it wasn't my fault, but it happened when I was right there. I feel like I should've stopped it, or prevented it."

He pulled up the wagon near the barn that was still standing. It was a small building, and it and the surrounding wooden fences had remained unharmed. Pattie jumped down and headed to the barn and Benjamin was quick to follow.

She turned around. "They're still here. I thought someone might have stolen them. This one is Chester and that one is Winnie."

Benjamin walked closer and looked them both over. "They look fine."

Pattie clipped a lead onto one horse and threw another lead over to Benjamin. He caught it and attached it to the other horse's halter. They led them out of the barn.

"I'll come back later and clean out their stalls," Benjamin said.

"Leave it. That's the least of my problems."

*"Nee,* I don't mind. I'd do it now, but I want to get these two back home and settled." He gently patted Chester's neck as he was leading him out.

WHEN PATTIE WAS HAVING a sleep that afternoon, Benjamin went back to her place to clean out the horses' stalls. When he got there, he did some general cleaning and reorganizing of the barn, and then turned his attention to the stalls.

As he worked, his mind traveled to Pattie. She'd been a kid when he'd left, now she was a young woman —an attractive young woman. He'd revised his first impression of her as still being a kid.

HE PROPPED the shovel against the wall, decided against

laying fresh straw not knowing when Pattie and the horses would be back, then he walked out of the barn. Two white vans were pulling up in front of the house. He walked closer and then waited while a man got out of the closest vehicle.

"Can I help you?" Benjamin asked.

"We're the investigation team."

There were around six of them, all in white suits. "Little late, aren't you? I thought you guys were supposed to investigate immediately after the event."

"There were no fatalities. We have to prioritize."

Benjamin nodded. "Ah, I understand. Well, I'll get out of your way."

As Benjamin was heading down the drive he met a police car, and the officer behind the wheel waved him down. His heart pounded in his chest. Police always made him nervous.

"Name?" the officer barked at him.

Benjamin recognized him as being one of the officers at the scene. "Benjamin Fuller. I was one of the volunteers here last night."

The officer looked at him blankly and then asked, "What are you doing here now?"

"Pattie, the girl who lived here, is staying with my folks. She wanted me to ... well, I offered to clean out the horse stalls. We moved her horses to my parents' barn earlier today for safekeeping and to make it easier to take care of them."

The officer grunted and then asked for Benjamin's

address and phone number, even though he'd already given it on Pattie's behalf. "We'll need to talk with Pattie again."

"She's pretty upset, and very tired. When I left home, she was asleep."

"We'll stop by later today."

It was then Benjamin saw another officer was in the passenger seat. "Okay. I'll tell her you'll be coming." Benjamin drove on with his heart still pounding.

WHEN HE ARRIVED HOME, he saw a much fresher-looking Pattie in a blue dress complete with white apron and a stiff white *kapp,* sitting by the fire keeping warm with his mother.

They both stopped talking and looked at him when he walked in the door.

"Pattie, there were some investigations in progress when I left your *haus* just now, and also the police were there. An officer said he's going to stop by later today and ask you more questions."

"They're coming here?" His mother looked horrified.

*"Jah, Mamm,* here."

She got off the couch. "I'll bake some cookies."

"I'll help, Mrs. Fuller."

*"Nee,* you sit and rest. I should've baked more yesterday. I was going to but I didn't."

When his mother left the room, Benjamin sat down with Pattie. "You look nice."

She looked down at her clothes. "This is Mary Lou's dress. She's such a fine sewer, just like you told me."

He cleared his throat. He hadn't meant the dress looked nice, he meant she did.

"I hope your *mudder* doesn't mind the police coming here."

He knew *Mamm* did mind. In fact, she'd be worried someone might see the police at the *haus.* What would people think? Not wanting Pattie to feel bad, he said, "She's worried she doesn't have anything to offer them to eat, which would be a first for her, and she'll solve that problem in short order. There's always too much to eat around here."

Pattie smiled and looked back at the fire. "I feel guilty sitting around not doing anything, but your *mudder* won't let me lift a finger."

"She likes doing things herself. It took her ages to allow my brothers' wives to help in the kitchen when we're having family dinners. That's just the way she is."

Pattie giggled. "She's funny, worrying about baking cookies for the officers. They aren't coming here to eat. It's not a social visit."

Benjamin nodded, and whether that was odd, or weird, that's just how his *Mamm* was. "Your horses look happy. I just saw them now."

"I know, I went out to take a look at them when you were gone. They like sharing that big stall. They've always been good friends. I'm so glad whoever it was burned the *haus* rather than the barn; they would've been locked in their stalls. We don't have a yard connected to the stalls like you do."

He could tell that she, like her brother, was fond of horses. "There's always something to be grateful for in a disaster. You didn't get hurt, so that was very good, too."

"I know."

"Can I get you anything, or do anything else for you?" he asked.

*"Nee.* You and your *mudder* have been so good already." She ran her hands over the lower part of her dress.

"Let me know if you think of anything."

"Well, there is one thing."

*"Jah?"* He was pleased she'd thought of something.

"Would you be able to drive me to work?"

"I'd be delighted. I can drive you there and collect you afterward."

# CHAPTER 6

PATTIE SAT in front of the officers after Mrs. Fuller had shown them into the house. Benjamin had left the house just before they arrived. She would've felt much better if he'd hung around. She realized she'd begun to find his presence calming.

The two uniformed officers were making an effort to be nice to her. She'd met both of them before at her home, after the fire was mostly out, but they'd reintroduced themselves to her as Constable Reynolds and Officer Hart..

Officer Hart pulled out a small notepad and pen. "Do you have any enemies?"

"No, I can't think of any enemies. I haven't got any, and neither does my brother."

"Would you mind coming to the station to have your fingerprints taken?" Reynolds asked.

"Now?"

"In the next couple of days would be fine."

She nodded.

"We found some prints and we want to eliminate yours," the constable explained.

"I could do that after work tomorrow."

"Give them your name at the desk when you get there, and they'll look after you."

"Okay."

"Is there anyone who would want you personally to suffer harm?"

She shook her head. "Not a single person."

"Tell us again what happened that day."

Pattie told them everything she had done, starting from when she woke in the morning. Then she ended with telling them she'd stayed up later than usual that evening, and was thinking it was time to head to bed. Then she'd heard a noise outside and had gone to investigate. Once she was outside, she told them, that was when she'd seen the flames. "And then I immediately called 911."

"And the house wasn't insured?"

"No."

"Would anyone stand to gain anything from destroying the house?"

"I can't think what anyone would gain."

Mrs. Fuller came bustling into the room with a tray of cookies and tea. "Would you gentlemen like hot tea and cookies?"

"Not for us, thanks."

She placed the tray down on the small table between the couches.

"I'll have one." Pattie reached out and took a cookie. She couldn't see Mrs. Fuller's efforts go to waste. She bit into it, and when she'd swallowed, she said, "You really should try these, they're delicious. The best cookies ever."

One of the officers looked at the cookies. "I'll have one. It wouldn't hurt. My wife's been trying to put me on a diet."

Mrs. Fuller said, "Yes, and I'll pour you all cups of tea." She stood between the officers and Pattie while she carefully poured the tea into cups through a tea strainer. "There you go and there's milk and sugar there too. Help yourself, unless you'd like me—"

"Thank you, Mrs. Fuller," Officer Hart said. "We'll manage from here."

"You're welcome." She stood with her hands clasped in front of her. "I'll leave you alone then, shall I?"

Pattie gave her a little smile and nodded.

When Mrs. Fuller was back in the kitchen, both officers took a few moments to stir sugar into their teas, and Hart added some milk to his. One grabbed two cookies, while the other officer, who was on a diet, stuck to one.

"I feel awful to know someone's done this deliberately. Do you think they were trying to harm me?"

"Has anything else happened?"

"No."

"Then it's unlikely. It could've been a prank. Something done by neighborhood kids."

"But, the house is so isolated. There aren't any of those types of kids around."

"We have those fingerprints. If the perpetrator has a record, his prints will be in the system."

Pattie nodded and nibbled on a cookie. She wouldn't feel safe until they got to the bottom of things.

# CHAPTER 7

THE NEXT MORNING, Benjamin and Pattie were sitting at the kitchen table eating breakfast with Mrs. Fuller when they all heard a thud.

Mrs. Fuller jumped in fright. "What was that?"

Benjamin got out of his chair. "I'll go see." Mr. Fuller had left for work earlier. Benjamin walked out the front door and lying directly in front of him on the ground was a bird.

"Oh how sad, is it dead?"

Benjamin looked around at Pattie, who'd followed him out. "I've seen birds do this before. I think they knock themselves out. If we give him some time, he might come around."

Pattie looked over her shoulder at the window. "He must've slammed into the window."

"Must have."

"Oh, but it's so cold out here. We can't just leave him on the cold ground. He'll freeze to death."

"I'll carry him to the barn so he'll be under cover, but where he'll be able to fly out when he comes around."

"Okay. What kind of bird is he?"

"Dunno. A brown one. Maybe a dove?"

"He's so pretty."

Benjamin carefully lifted the bird, walked over to the barn and laid him down on a bale of hay. "This is close enough to the door for the bird to find his way out."

"What about cats?"

"We don't have any. He'll be safe in here and hidden enough from any other predators."

"I hope so."

"Let's go back inside. I'll check on him later when I hitch the buggy." Benjamin was certain the bird was dead, but he didn't want to upset Pattie by saying so. He'd remove the bird later and tell Pattie it had flown away.

As they walked back to the house, she said, *"Denke* for driving me to work."

He chuckled, "I haven't done it yet."

"I'm thanking you in advance."

"What else would I do today? I've got no work yet and the whole day stretched before me until the men can have a look at your house. Then, we'll all help rebuild it and that'll keep me busy and give me something to do. I told you, out of disasters good things can come."

"Like giving you something to do with all your free time?"

"That's right. Let's finish our breakfast."

"You're funny, Benjamin."

Benjamin didn't know if he wanted Pattie to find him funny. Adorable, maybe, or handsome. Yes, that would be better. She was younger than other girls he'd been attracted to. Was this love he was feeling, or was he simply feeling protective of Pattie as he would feel toward a younger sister, if he'd ever had one?

Benjamin washed his hands in the mudroom and, as he sat back down at the table, he heard Pattie telling his mother about the bird.

"You think the bird will recover?" His mother's pinched expression told Benjamin she knew what he was up to.

He nodded. "Quite possibly. I've seen birds recover from flying into windows."

*Mamm* gave him a look. Was it disappointment he saw in her eyes? Then she said to Pattie, "Don't get your hopes up. The bird might be dead."

He frowned at his mother. How could she say something like that to a sweet girl like Pattie? She should know nothing of death or disappointment. Then he realized Pattie had seen much of both in her young life. Both parents were gone. Her house had burned down, leaving her homeless, and her brother had moved away before that, leaving her all alone. Time to change the topic of conversation. "What do you do at work, Pattie?"

"Ah, well, anything they want me to do. Sometimes, I'll do the washing, but mostly I clean and make up the rooms. In the high season, they put on more cleaners and that's mostly when I'm needed to do different jobs. I prefer to answer the phone and make the bookings, that's what I do in the summer, but it's not so busy this time of year."

"And where is it you work?" his mother asked.

"At the bed and breakfast at the end of Glenbrook Drive."

"Ah, it used to be owned by Ted and Izzy Graber."

Pattie nodded. "The current owners are *Englischers* and they've owned it for two years."

Mrs. Fuller asked, "Are they good to work for?"

*"Jah,* very *gut."*

Benjamin stood. He had to get back to the bird and do something with it before Pattie went outside. "I'll hitch the buggy and wait for you outside. Don't hurry."

"Okay."

As he pulled the front door open and stepped onto the porch, he figured he should give the bird the best chance it could have. He'd move it over to the other side of the barn out of Pattie's sight.

When Benjamin came to the spot he'd placed the bird, it had gone. He chuckled to himself and was pleased he didn't have to make up a story. The bird had just been knocked out, after all. A quick look around showed him no feathers, and no sign of stray cats, dogs, or foxes, which told him the bird had recovered.

SEVERAL MINUTES LATER, Pattie climbed into the waiting buggy and placed a black coat over her legs.

"The bird's gone," Benjamin said.

"Really? It's okay?"

*"Jah,* it must be. When I came to check on it, it wasn't there."

"I'm so glad."

He clicked his horse onward.

"When you went back to my barn yesterday, did you bring any feed over?"

*"Nee* we have plenty. A whole winter's worth of food. Don't worry about that or anything else."

"I'll have a lot to repay."

*"Nee,* not necessary. Zach is coming sometime today. He'll be here by the time you finish work."

"I can't wait to see him. I hope he's not going to be too upset."

"He'll be pleased that you're unharmed."

"I guess."

They trotted on in silence for a few minutes. Benjamin was enjoying Pattie's company. Pattie was different than other women. The women he dated were out to impress him, and Pattie was just being herself. Although, she probably didn't see him as anything more than a friend. Right there, right then, Benjamin knew he had to have her notice him as a man, and not just a friend of her brother.

"We're a little early," she said as they approached the bed and breakfast.

"It doesn't hurt to start early, does it?"

"I guess not."

"I'll be waiting right here when you finish. Um, what time will that be?"

"Three."

"I'll be here before three."

*"Denke,* Benjamin." She climbed down from the buggy.

When she was out of sight, he moved his horse back onto the road and headed home in silence. During the process of unhitching the buggy, the phone rang. He answered it and was surprised it was Zach, who should've been arriving shortly.

"Benjamin, I can't get there until Saturday."

"Pattie will be disappointed."

"I know, but I've got loose ends to tie up here and people are relying on me. It's not urgent, is it?"

*"Nee,* there are decisions to make regarding the rebuilding, but I guess they won't take place until you get here unless they're things Pattie is comfortable deciding."

"How is she?"

"She's pretending to be strong, but I can see she's

really upset. She's homeless, and she feels responsible, and also guilty."

"Sorry, I've got to go. Tell her it's okay and I'll be there Saturday, would you?"

"Yeah, I will."

"And thank your parents for having her stay, and letting me stay there too."

"It's fine. I will."

Zach ended the call. Benjamin hung up the receiver, not wanting to give the bad news to Pattie. She'd been looking forward to her brother's arrival. He hadn't even asked Zach what time he'd be there on Saturday.

## CHAPTER 8

BENJAMIN GOT to Pattie's place of work early and parked just off the road close by. It was nice to sit quietly by himself away from his mother's constant questions. Traveling by himself the past years had given him many life experiences—some good and some bad. His thoughts led him to the women who'd been in his life. They'd all expected marriage and it was their desperation that he had found off-putting. Pattie was refreshing. If he didn't marry her, he'd marry someone exactly like her; someone who was natural and normal, who wasn't hard work to be around.

She'd been at work all day and he hadn't been able to get her out of his mind. If he dated her and things didn't work out, he'd feel dreadful to hurt her. But wait, what if she ended up hurting him? There was always the possibility things would end well, which would be a marvelous outcome, but none of his relationships had in the past.

To save his sanity and get away from the jumbled thoughts rolling around in his head, he jumped down from the buggy, and then walked up and down hoping Pattie wouldn't be too upset that her brother was delayed. When a gust of chilling wind swept along the road, he pulled his coat tighter around himself. Just as he was about to retreat to the warmth of the buggy, Pattie came into view wrapped in a black coat—most likely one of his mother's—that was way too big for her. He stood there and watched with a pounding heart as a smile met her lips.

"Is he here?" she asked as she rushed to him.

He'd momentarily forgotten his bad news. "He called and said he won't be here now until Saturday."

"Why's that?"

Benjamin shrugged. "Something to do with his work. He couldn't talk for long. I'm so sorry, Pattie." He couldn't bear it if she was too upset.

"That's okay, I'll be alright. At least he's coming back on Saturday. What time—"

He grimaced. "I forgot to ask what time. All I know is Saturday."

When they were both in the buggy, she said, "Oh, Benjamin, I've got to do the fingerprinting for the police. I told them I'd come after work."

He'd forgotten it, and he would've preferred if she'd forgotten it also. He didn't want to go anywhere near the police. He'd had one or two experiences with them and knew they weren't all helpful and friendly as he'd once believed. He fixed a smile on his face, as he glanced over at her. "We'll go there now."

*"Denke.* That will be one more thing off my mind."

He continued into town and parked the buggy as close as he could to the police station. Hoping she'd say 'no,' he asked, "Do you want me to come in with you?"

*"Jah,* please come with me."

"Okay." He gritted his teeth and got out of the buggy.

ONCE INSIDE THE POLICE STATION, Pattie was shown to a room where she was fingerprinted. The whole process only took fifteen minutes and then she was free to go.

~

ON SATURDAY, Benjamin was on the porch waiting with Pattie when Zach's taxi came into view. He'd gotten a taxi from the bus station.

Pattie ran to the vehicle as soon as it stopped. Benjamin moved to the edge of the porch and watched the reunion. Zach hugged his younger sister, and when the taxi drove away, Benjamin walked over. He waited until they'd finished saying words to each other, then Benjamin offered his hand and Zach shook it.

Zach said, "*Denke* for looking after Pattie."

"Not me, it's *Mamm.*" Benjamin chuckled and then grabbed Zach's suitcase from by his feet.

"I can do that," Zach said.

"I'm sure you can. You go on into the *haus* with Pattie. *Mamm's* been waiting all day for you to arrive. There'll be someone else in the *haus* she can fatten up."

"Yeah, Zach, Mrs. Fuller's a *wunderbaar* cook."

"I'll look forward to tasting her cooking. I've been fending for myself these past months." He shook his head. "I can't believe what's happened."

"Have you seen what's left of our *haus* yet?"

"*Nee,* we didn't drive that way. Is it really bad?"

Pattie nodded. "There's barely anything left."

"Let's get in out of the cold." Benjamin led the way, carrying Zach's suitcase, and showed Zach where his bedroom was. His mother had Zach in the bedroom next to Pattie's. When Benjamin set the suitcase down, he said, "My *mudder* has made a roast."

"I might never leave," Zach said with a grin.

Pattie added, "She's been keeping it warm because we weren't sure what time you'd get here."

"Don't hurry, get comfortable and I'll see you in the kitchen." Benjamin walked out and left brother and sister to talk. Then he realized his mother hadn't come out to greet Zach. He found her in the kitchen stirring something on the stove. Looking over her shoulder, he saw it was gravy. "Zach's here, *Mamm.*"

"*Jah,* I know, but the gravy won't wait."

"He's in his room. He'll be down in a moment."

She stopped stirring and stared at him. "How long is a moment?"

"I told him there was no hurry."

She shook her head. "The meal will be ready in three minutes. Can you fetch our guests now?"

"Okay." Benjamin headed back up the stairs feeling like a fool. He'd just told them there was no hurry. *Mamm* got annoyed if people were tardy coming to the table. He stuck his head through the doorway. "Previously, I said to take your time, but after checking with the lady of the house, I'm told that good gravy waits for no man."

Zach and Pattie laughed. "We're ready right now," Zach said.

Benjamin rubbed his chin. "Please tell me you haven't eaten already."

"I'm starving." Zach patted his stomach.

"Phew! That'll make *Mamm* happy."

When Zach walked into the kitchen, Mrs. Fuller, greeted him and told him he and Pattie were welcome to stay as long as they wanted.

"We're grateful, I can tell you that much. *Denke* for your kindness, and you too, Benjamin. You were one of the volunteers, Pattie told me."

"That's right. I've been doing that for years, since I left here."

Since it was mid-afternoon when the meal was over, Benjamin asked Zach, "Would you like to go with me to Isaac's *haus,* so we can get your input on the rebuild?"

"Oh, Benjamin," Mrs. Fuller said, "He's only just arrived. Give him a chance to rest."

Zach smiled. "That's fine, Mrs Fuller, I'm happy to get started with everything as soon as I possibly can."

"Well, don't overdo it. You've had a long journey."

"I feel much better now after that meal."

"You just needed some good food in you." Mrs. Fuller leaned over and patted him on his hand.

Benjamin had forgotten how his mother liked to look after everybody. At times, though, she was a little forceful. "We'll try not to stress him too much."

"Can I come too?" Pattie asked.

"Of course you can," Benjamin said.

"Can you wait until I help with the dishes?"

"Go now," Mrs. Fuller said. "There's not much to do. I'm used to being alone in the kitchen anyway. That's where I do my best thinking.

"Are you sure?"

Mrs. Fuller nodded. *"Jah."*

Benjamin then had the sorry task of showing Zach what had become of his and Pattie's house.

## CHAPTER 9

MARY LOU WAS uncomfortable at the Sunday meeting. Magnolia, who was sitting next to her, kept turning and staring at the two women who'd married James and Gabe, the widowers she'd told Magnolia about on her last visit. From the look on Magnolia's face she was angry with the poor women. Had she really expected one of those men to wait for her, even though they knew nothing about her?

The problem that Mary Lou faced was who to suggest to Magnolia now. Zach had returned because his family home had burned down, but he'd soon be gone again. The other possibility was Magnolia's man she'd recently broken up with. Would he have her back? With a little coaching, she could teach Magnolia to keep her mouth and her temper under control. Surely that would be the quickest and easiest way for

Magnolia to get married. After all, the man must've liked her to be courting her for months.

As soon as Magnolia brought the subject up again, which wouldn't be long, Mary Lou would suggest she call or write to her old boyfriend. Mary Lou looked down at her youngest in Magnolia's arms. Although Magnolia was difficult to get along with and had a one-of-a-kind personality, she showed great patience with children. That indicated she would make a good mother, if some man was willing to give her a chance.

Magnolia was still twisting and leaning to one side.

"Do you want me to take Jimmy from you?" Mary Lou asked.

"*Nee,* I'm fine. He's fast asleep."

"Why do you keep craning your neck and looking up that way?"

"I'm looking at those women who married James and Gabe. You didn't

tell me they were both pregnant."

"Didn't I? I was certain I had."

"*Nee* you didn't, and I'm understandably very upset about that."

"About what?"

"It should've been me. I should've married one of them and it would've been me having a *boppli.* Soon, I'll be too old to have one. The chances of getting pregnant lessen a lot after thirty, you know."

Mary Lou couldn't help being a little annoyed. "Last

time you were here, I suggested both Gabe and James, and you turned your nose up at them."

"That's not right. I was interested. Anyway, there's no point arguing about it now." She scanned the congregation. "I want to know which of the men are single."

Still annoyed, Mary Lou sat straight in her chair and looked ahead. "The clean-shaven ones."

"Silly, not which ones aren't married, that much's obvious. Which ones don't have a girlfriend? I don't want to waste my time being nice to a man only to find out he's courting someone."

"You've got to spend time getting to know somebody first."

"I'll get to know him once we're married."

Mary Lou cringed. "That strategy could be a bit risky."

"Right now, the only thing I'm risking is being an old maid, and that's not something I want."

"Me either."

"What are you talking about? You have Jacob."

Mary Lou sighed. Magnolia was such hard work. Why couldn't she have stayed with someone else? "I mean, that's not what I want for you. Pattie's *bruder,* Zach, is here somewhere. I saw him before. Jacob told me he got back yesterday to help rebuild his family home."

"Where?"

"I'll look for him when the meeting's finished. I'll introduce you to him."

Magnolia's face lit up. "Okay. You said he's got light hair?"

*"Jah."*

"I see someone like that." From their back row seat, Magnolia craned her neck again trying to look around people, and Mary Lou took Jimmy back and settled him across her lap.

With the children, it was easier for Mary Lou to sit near a door in case she had to take one of them outside. Now she had thoughts of taking Magnolia outside. Mary Lou hissed, "Here comes one of the deacons."

Jeremiah Hilty stepped to the front of the room and opened the meeting in prayer. With her eyes tightly closed, Mary Lou hoped that Magnolia would keep quiet throughout the service. Keeping Magnolia quiet was worse than keeping her three children quiet, and they didn't know any better.

"I see Pattie, but where is he? You know if I have one more disappointment ..."

"Shh."

Throughout the course of the meeting, Mary Lou had to hush Magnolia three times, dig her in the ribs twice and step on her foot once. By the end of it, Mary Lou was nearly exhausted and she was glad it was over. She hadn't even been able to concentrate on the bishop's words when he'd been delivering the sermon.

Magnolia and Mary Lou remained seated while

everyone moved out of the Bylers' house. Mary Lou's baby had gone back to sleep and his siblings were looking like they were about to sleep, too. Jacob approached and kindly took the older two, giving her a sympathetic smile. The whole time, Magnolia had been having a good look at everyone.

"I think I see him," Magnolia said when Jacob had gone.

"Good. Let's get out of the house and I'll introduce you."

Magnolia looked down at Jimmy. "Are you okay with the *boppli?*"

*"Jah,* I can manage."

*"Nee,* give him to me." Magnolia didn't wait for a response, she leaned over and took the sleeping baby out of his mother's arms.

Mary Lou stood, pleased that her aching arms could have a rest.

When they walked out of the *haus* and down the steps into the makeshift undercover area that was being warmed by heaters, Mary Lou nodded toward a young man. "That's him over there, talking to Peter Willis."

"Ah, I thought that was him."

"Let's go."

Magnolia gave a nervous giggle. "I don't know. I'm not good at meeting new people."

Mary Lou looked at her cousin's nervous face. She was normally bolder. "Just be yourself."

"Being myself has never worked for me before."

Mary Lou giggled. No truer words had come out of Magnolia's mouth. "Be the best version of yourself."

"Okay, I'll try. You take the *boppli* back, though, or he might think I'm married."

"At least my arms have had a little rest."

"I'll take him from you again soon."

# CHAPTER 10

MARY LOU NODDED and headed toward Zach. Zach stopped talking to Peter and moved toward the two women.

"Hi, Mary Lou."

"Hello, Zach. I'm so sorry about your *haus*."

"Oh well, can't do much about it now. Everyone's helping to rebuild it. And, thank you for the clothes you've given my *schweschder*."

"That was nothing. I've got plenty."

His gaze fell to the baby. "He was only a few days old when I left."

Magnolia poked Mary Lou in the back.

"Oh, Zach, this is my cousin, Magnolia."

Zach's face lighted up.

"Hello, Magnolia. I've seen you through the years while you've been visiting your cousin."

She smiled at him. "You remember me?"

*"Jah.* You've been here about three times that I remember."

Magnolia inched closer to him. "Mary Lou tells me that you moved away?"

*"Jah,* I moved to work with a friend of mine in Unionville. He's got several business interests and he wanted me to help manage them."

"Wanted?" Mary Lou said, "Does that mean you might come back?"

"I don't know. I feel awful leaving Pattie here alone, but I love my job. I'm torn."

"What does your friend do?" Magnolia asked.

"Everything to do with horse racing. He owns a track, and trades horses on the side, imports the buggies and alters them. He's got interests in everything to do with racing. The bishop here isn't so … well, he's not so much in favor of racing."

Each community had its differences from the others; some activities were frowned upon in some and not in others. The bishop didn't mind them watching, he just didn't like them racing, and naturally, betting on the races was forbidden.

Joshua joined them and told Mary Lou that the older two children were down for a nap in one of the Bylers' bedrooms.

"I love racing," Magnolia said.

Zach smiled. "Do you?"

*"Jah."*

"There's a race on this weekend if you'd like to come with me."

"Really? I'd like to come."

"We should all go," Joshua said.

"You'll be racing in it?" Mary Lou asked Zach.

*"Nee,* just watching. I have a friend of mine who's racing."

Mary Lou would have a quiet word with Jacob. He hadn't picked up that she was trying to match Magnolia with Zach. Magnolia was doing a good job hiding her annoyance at Joshua for inviting himself and Mary Lou. Zach had directed that question at Magnolia and there had been no mistaking that.

"We'll all be there, won't we?" Jacob asked looking at Mary Lou and Magnolia.

Mary Lou gave a polite nod, wondering how the little ones would behave at a horse race. Maybe she could leave the older two with Ivy for the day.

Magnolia said, "I'd love to go."

"Good." Zach smiled at her. "I'll be at your place at eight in the morning, Jacob, and you can follow me there."

"Sounds good. We'll be waiting," Jacob said, still unaware he was butting in. Jacob started talking to Zach about the details of rebuilding his house, and Magnolia and Mary Lou walked away.

"Did you hear that?" Magnolia whispered. "I'll take the *boppli* now."

Mary Lou handed him over. "I did, and I'm so sorry that Jacob had no idea what was happening."

"Was I wrong, or did Zach only invite me?"

"I honestly think he did. That's the way it sounded to me."

"Oh, Mary Lou, Saturday is too far away for me to see him again." She turned around to take another look at him. "He's so handsome and seems like such a nice person."

*"Jah,* he truly is. Be patient, Magnolia. Let things happen naturally, in their own time."

As they walked closer to a spare table, Magnolia said, "Time is my enemy. Too much time has passed already. I'll never be happy until I'm married." She looked down at Jimmy. "With my own *boppli,* or two, or even three just like you."

"They're staying at Ivy's and Ivy's not having any more family dinners while they're there, so I don't see how—"

"I need a plan." Magnolia passed Jimmy back to Mary Lou.

Mary Lou grimaced. Magnolia's plans never ended well. "Just let *Gott* do his work."

"He is working, through me. He's just given me a *gut* plan, and I must carry it out."

Mary Lou sighed and repositioned her sleeping baby over her shoulder. "What is it?"

"If I make friends with Celia, I'll find out how she trapped Gabe."

Mary Lou giggled until she saw Magnolia's serious face. "Are you going to do that, really?"

"Yeah. I'm going to go talk to Celia now." Magnolia nodded to the other side of the food table where Celia was alone and heaping food on her plate. "She's at the food table by herself. It's a perfect opportunity."

## CHAPTER 11

MAGNOLIA WAS in no mood to listen to more of her cousin's negativity. She stared at Celia and figured she was no beauty, so she wasn't quite certain what Gabe saw in her. Hopefully, she'd learn a few secrets. "Hello, Celia."

Celia put her plate down on the table and turned to look at Magnolia. "Hello. You're Mary Lou's cousin, aren't you?"

"That's right." Magnolia's gaze lowered to Celia's large belly. "You're expecting?"

"Yeah, I have only three months to go."

"That explains why you're putting so much food on your plate. You're eating for two."

Celia looked down at her plate. "Oh, does it look like too much?"

*"Nee,* eat up. That's so lovely you're married and you married . . . ?"

"Gabe, and now we're about to have our third."

Magnolia frowned. "But the other two aren't yours; they were from his first marriage, weren't they?"

Celia gave a little giggle. "That's right. And they are both of ours now, since we're married."

"Hmm. Technically, I suppose you could say that." Magnolia reminded herself to be friendlier. "I'm so happy for you."

*"Denke,* that's thoughtful."

"And do you work outside the house? Oh, don't let me stop you getting food now that you're eating for two." Magnolia picked up an empty plate from the end of the table and started helping herself to the food.

Celia picked up her plate. "I'm the schoolteacher."

"You are?"

"That's right."

"I always wanted to be a schoolteacher. Are you going to continue after you have the *boppli?"*

*"Nee,* that would be far too much work for me with the three *kinner*. The older one is such a help to me, but she's still young and I don't want to put too much pressure on her."

*"Jah,* and she might resent you since you're not her real *mudder."*

"Well, I am now. I'm her *mudder."*

*"Jah,* okay." Magnolia coughed and said, under her breath, "Not really." She then licked her lips. "Tell me, Celia. Who's going to take over from you in your teaching job?"

"They have a replacement arriving from Reading."

"Really? Couldn't they find anyone in this community to do the job? I thought there'd be plenty who'd want a teaching job."

"Apparently not. None that the board approved of anyway."

"It must be very fulfilling to be a teacher."

"It is, but sometimes it's not very easy. It can be very demanding. It's like juggling a dozen balls in the air at one time and making sure you catch them all. All the children are on different levels and you have to stay on top of everything."

"Sounds easy to me. I love children."

"Maybe you'd like to help out sometime? I could use an extra pair of hands and another set of eyes."

"I sure would. I'd love to. Maybe I should become a teacher."

"You could be one if you wanted to."

"I was always very good at school." Magnolia stopped herself from saying any more. It wasn't good to boast, and she wanted to make a good impression on Celia. Remembering that she wanted to get to know Celia better to discover her secrets, she asked, "Would I be able to help out soon? I've got loads of free time on my hands."

"How about tomorrow?"

"Oh, could I?"

"*Jah*, I'd love your help."

"Great. What time should I be there?"

"How does nine-thirty sound?"

"Perfect. I'm looking forward to knowing exactly what the job entails. When does your replacement come?"

"She should've been here by now. She was due to start tomorrow, but she's delayed it to next Monday."

"That is a week away."

"I know. She hasn't shown herself to be reliable so far."

"Maybe I could do the job."

Celia smiled. "Rebecca has the job, but if something happens, you should definitely apply for it."

"I will. I'll definitely be there tomorrow. *Denke.* I can't wait to tell Mary Lou."

"You're doing me and the students a big favor. The children react well to a new face. I'm sure they're bored with having me teach them all the time."

"I'm curious about something and it's a personal question, so don't answer if you don't want to."

"What is it?"

"What's it like being married to someone who's been married before?"

"I don't really know any different, but I have to be mindful and respectful of Gabe and the children's memories of her, and things like that."

"You have to be sensitive?"

"That's right."

Then and there, Magnolia knew she wouldn't be a good candidate for marrying a widower. She would surely put her foot in it and offend people some way or other. Magnolia continued to pile food on her plate, staying close to Celia.

"How long are you here for, Magnolia?"

"I'm not sure. I haven't been here in about five years. This is the first time I've seen Mary Lou's *kinner*. I can't believe how all the community has changed in these past few years and all the new faces here."

Celia giggled. "Me included."

"Yeah, where did you come from?"

"I came from Walnut Creek, Ohio. I came over here for my *onkel's* funeral, and that's when I met Gabe."

*"Jah,* funerals are a *gut* way to meet people."

Celia giggled as though Magnolia was making a joke, but Magnolia was dead serious.

"And was it love at first sight?" Magnolia asked.

"Not at first sight, *nee,* but we really liked each other once we got talking. And then we wrote to each other for about six months and then he proposed in a letter."

Magnolia was so envious she felt like she'd been kicked in the stomach. Trying to hide it, she commented, "How romantic."

*"Jah,* it was."

"That's *wunderbaar* for you."

*"Jah."* Celia stepped away from the table and Magnolia fell in line with her.

"Where are you going to sit?" Magnolia asked, sure she had a lot she could learn from the recently married woman.

Celia looked around. "I can't see Gabe anywhere and the kids are playing, no doubt."

"Sit with me, then. We can sit right here."

Together they sat at the first spare table. Magnolia's plan to get to know her was going well.

After Magnolia ate a mouthful, she continued her small talk. "Families can be difficult sometimes. Do you get along with all of your husband's family?"

"I do. I think they were just so happy that he found somebody to love again."

"They would be, I guess. It's not easy to find someone to love. I've been looking for a long time. I had some longish relationships, but they went nowhere. I ended the last one, because he was taking too long to ask me to marry him. I didn't think he was serious." Magnolia shrugged and cut a piece of chicken and popped it into her mouth.

"Love isn't easy sometimes that's for sure and for certain. That's why I began teaching. I had a few disappointments early on and I just thought love wasn't meant for me."

"And did teaching help?"

"It kept my mind off my sorrowful thoughts." Celia gave a little giggle.

Magnolia remembered her old teacher, Miss Shwetz. She'd never married and she had seemed happy enough. Maybe teaching was her answer. Had *Gott* led her to Celia so she could take a new path—a path that was man-free and disappointment-free?

# CHAPTER 12

THE NEXT MORNING, Magnolia borrowed one of Jacob and Mary Lou's buggies.

"You're going to help out at the school?"

"I am. Celia and I have become quite good friends."

"Have you found out her secret yet?" Mary Lou couldn't keep in her giggle.

"I don't think she has a secret. They just met and it happened just so easily. I wish that would happen for me but it happened unexpectedly for her. When she wasn't looking for love, love found her. I wonder if it will happen that way for me. Probably not, because I'm always looking."

"It seems such a good idea, though, to take your mind off things by helping others."

"Helping who?" Magnolia asked.

"The school children."

"Oh, yes, them."

"What will you be doing exactly?"

"I have no idea. Teaching them history, math, spelling, things like that I guess. That should be easy enough."

"Are you going to be there all day?"

"I don't know, she didn't say. Probably not all day." Magnolia decided then and there she wasn't going to stay all day. "I better go, or I'll be late."

"Have a good day, Magnolia."

Magnolia kissed Adam and Lucinda, who were playing on a rug on the kitchen floor, and then tried to leave. Lucinda her niece, cried when she walked away.

Magnolia turned back and sat cross-legged on the rug. "Lucinda, you can't come with me. I have a job today. It's a teaching job. When you're older, you'll go to school."

"Me too," Adam said.

"That's right. Even little Jimmy will. Now, you stay home with your big *bruder, Mamm* and Jimmy. Okay?" When Magnolia got up to go, she cried again. Magnolia looked over at Mary Lou for help.

"She likes food. Give her a cookie and she'll let you go."

"That's a dreadful habit to give her."

Mary Lou giggled. "We'll break her of it later, but right now don't you need to leave?"

"Good point." Magnolia grabbed the cookie jar and gave one each to Adam and Lucinda. When the children were occupied with their cookies, she grabbed her belongings and ran out the door. Once she'd closed the door, she pulled on her coat and then rammed her black over-bonnet over her white prayer *kapp*.

She wasn't too keen on early February mornings in the bitter cold. It would've been nicer to sit by the fire and work on her sampler. That's what she thought she'd be doing at Mary Lou's place. That and meeting eligible bachelors, but Mary Lou was failing miserably in that department unless something came from meeting Zach. Jacob had already hitched the buggy for her and she was thankful for that.

She trotted the horse to the one-room schoolhouse, feeling pleased with herself. Now, she'd see exactly what being a teacher was all about. When she arrived, she saw all the children disappearing in the doorway. "So much for being early. *Denke,* Lucinda. Just as well you like cookies." She secured the buggy right next to one she figured must've been Celia's and then hurried into the classroom.

School had just started back after a short winter break, and it was cold for February.

There were a group of students crowded around Celia, and Magnolia made her way through them.

Before Magnolia could tell Celia that she could only stay for a couple of hours, Celia hushed all the children. "Everyone, this is Miss Magnolia."

"Good morning, Miss Magnolia," the children chanted.

"Good morning, everyone," Magnolia replied putting on her best smile.

"Miss Magnolia is going to be helping out today."

"Um, only part of the day, I'm afraid. I forgot I had a prior arrangement."

"Part of the day is good. We better get started." Celia clapped her hands loudly and the children hurried to sit behind their desks.

Magnolia hoped she wouldn't be bored. If there was one thing she could not cope with, it was boredom.

Celia had the children write out their times tables, different ones for different ages. Magnolia made her way around the class helping the children who were struggling. She told the children little tricks she'd learned to help her remember. After that, there were mathematical problems that the older children had to figure out, while the younger ones concentrated on their spelling.

Magnolia could see why Celia was grateful to have an extra pair of hands.

When the children were on their mid morning break, Magnolia seized the opportunity to gain an older woman's advice. "Celia, I like Zach and he invited me to the horse racing yesterday after the meeting and then Jacob overheard and invited himself and other people along. At first, I was cranky, but then I thought it might work out better that way."

"It could. It's good that he invited you. He would be

upset also that Jacob thought the invitation extended to him."

"I hope so."

"I'm sure he would've."

"Now I have to put up with everyone being there. How do I get any of Zach's attention?"

"If he asked you, he will give you the attention."

"That's right. I didn't think of that. You're good at this."

Celia laughed.

"Unfortunately," Magnolia continued, even though Celia's eyes glazed over, "I have had a lot of failures in relationships and they haven't always been my fault."

"Ah."

Magnolia leaned closer. "What do you mean?"

Blinking rapidly, Celia said, "Um, nothing. I'm just listening."

"Oh, I thought you saw something wrong with me."

Celia breathed out heavily. "There's nothing, you just need to relax. You remind me of how I used to be."

Magnolia slowly nodded wondering whether that was good or bad. It was good, she decided, because Celia was now married.

## CHAPTER 13

ON THE WAY home from school, Magnolia thought she would be a good teacher. It was a way of spending all day with children. Now she faced the rest of the day with Mary Lou. Perhaps it might have been more interesting to stay at school. Then Magnolia had a better idea.

When Magnolia got back to Mary Lou's house, she didn't unhitch the buggy, she went inside to see what Mary Lou thought of part two of her plan.

She found Mary Lou sitting on the couch feeding the baby.

Magnolia sat down next to her cousin. "How many times a day do you feed Jimmy?"

"As often as he wants. He sleeps plenty, so it's okay."

"Oh. I've had an idea."

She noticed Mary Lou took a quick breath of air.

"Don't worry, it's a good one. If I become friends with Pattie, then I'll see more of Zach."

Mary Lou sighed. "At this rate, Magnolia, you'll have a lot of fake friends. People who think they're your friends, but you're using them. Like you're using Celia."

Magnolia's jaw dropped open. "I just spent all day helping her do her job, and I was working for free. Who's using who, hmmm?"

"We both know why you're friends with her. You told me so yourself."

"But they can become my friends. I've already developed a bond with Celia. I think Pattie needs all the friends she can get right now. Do you want to visit her with me? I'll help you look after the little ones."

"*Nee,* I'm a little tired."

"Can I borrow the buggy again, then?"

"*Jah,* of course. Did you enjoy your time at the school?"

"*Wunderbaar*. I want to become a teacher if my romantic life doesn't work out."

"Okay."

"Teaching is my backup plan." She jumped to her feet. "Can I borrow some of your clothes? I want to make the best impression."

"Sure. Take whatever you want."

Fifteen minutes later, and wearing borrowed clothes, Magnolia headed for the front door and yelled over her shoulder, "Gotta go. Be home later." Magnolia was pleased to get away from Mary Lou and be by herself, at least for the short ride in the buggy. She was also aware that Zach was staying with Obadiah and Ivy Fuller.

~

BENJAMIN WAS NOW the only son living at the Fullers' home, and if God smiled on her today, she'd arrive at the house and only Zach would be there.

She giggled as she thought what she'd say to Zach. She'd taken great pains to get ready and had even shined her black boots and changed the shoelaces for new ones. The prayer *kapp* and apron she wore were sheer organza. Mary Lou always had the best clothing and it was good that she didn't mind her borrowing them.

When Magnolia got to the bottom of the Fullers' long driveway, she saw a man near their barn. Hoping it was Zach, and hoping for a quiet word alone, she wasted no time trotting her horse up for a closer look.

It was Zach. He stood there waiting for her near a horse and buggy, and he didn't look happy.

"Hello, Zach."

"Hi, Magnolia." He walked over and helped her secure her horse.

"Are you going somewhere?" she asked.

He looked over at the waiting buggy. "*Nee,* I've just

hitched it for Mrs. Fuller. She's going somewhere. What are you doing here?"

"I've come to visit your *schweschder.* Is she home?"

"*Jah,* she is."

"What's the matter? You don't look very happy."

He placed his hands on his hips. "I'm upset about the *haus.* My parents left us both money and I was hoping it would be enough to rebuild it, but it isn't. It won't go near to covering the materials. I was just going for a walk to let off some steam."

"That's a good idea."

He gave her a nod. "Pattie's in the *haus* somewhere."

"I'll find her."

He walked behind the barn, and once he was out of sight, Magnolia followed him. She stood at the corner of the barn, so she could quickly duck away if he turned back around. Then she saw him pick up a large stone and he drew his arm back and flung it at a tree. He didn't stop there. He walked over and kicked the tree. Not once, but three times!

With her heart pumping hard, Magnolia moved away. Now she was more attracted to him than ever. He had a temper just like hers. This had to be a perfect match and she had to have him.

"Magnolia!"

Magnolia heard Pattie's voice and then saw her waving to her from the porch. She waved back and quickly walked over to her, not wanting Zach to suspect she'd been watching.

"What were you doing, Maggie?"

Magnolia bristled when she heard that name. She'd always hated it. "I was just wondering where your *bruder* was going."

"For a walk, he said."

"Hmm." Magnolia continued walking toward her.

"What are you doing here?" she asked, sort of repeating herself.

Magnolia fixed a smile on her face. "I'm here to visit you."

"Great!" When Magnolia stepped onto the porch, Pattie looked her up and down. "Oh, you look so pretty today."

That compliment made up for calling her Maggie. Almost. Magnolia touched the prayer *kapp.* "I've borrowed some of Mary Lou's clothes."

"What's the special occasion?"

"Visiting you and Mrs. Fuller, of course."

Pattie giggled. "I was just trying to help Mrs. Fuller bake bread, but she doesn't like anyone helping her, I've found out. The bread's just come out of the oven. Can you smell it?"

Magnolia breathed in the aroma of the freshly baked bread. "I sure can."

"It's the best smell, when it's just come out of the oven. She said to ask you if you want hot tea or *kaffe.*"

"Hmm, *kaffe* would be nice."

"She's just put the kettle on. Let's go." Pattie grabbed Magnolia's hand and led her further into the house.

Mrs. Fuller was fixing mugs in a row when Magnolia walked into the kitchen. "Hello, Mrs. Fuller."

"Ah, Magnolia, it's nice to see you again. Why don't you girls stay and chat? I've got a friend who's not well and I need to take her some bread and soup."

"I'll make the *kaffe,"* Pattie said.

Mrs. Fuller said, *"Nee,* you sit and I'll make it for you. What would you like, Magnolia, a hot drink to warm you, or perhaps a lemonade?"

"We'd both like *kaffe* please," Pattie said.

Once the girls had drinks in front of them, Mrs. Fuller packed her basket and left to run her errands.

"It's nice that your *bruder* has come back to help rebuild the *haus,"* Magnolia said.

*"Jah,* well, it's half his."

"Does he have a ... a friend?"

"What's that? A female friend?"

"Yeah." Magnolia had to find out to save wasting time.

"You should've just said a girlfriend, then." Pattie giggled. "You're so funny, Maggie."

Magnolia didn't like being laughed at any better than she liked that name. "Don't call me Maggie. I don't like it when people call me that."

"Okay Mags, Magpie. Is that why you always wear black and white? Magpie. Do you also collect shiny objects?" Pattie giggled again.

Although Magnolia was taking a dislike to Pattie,

she reminded herself to be nice to her. If she married Zach, Pattie would be her sister-in-law.

"People call me Pattie, short for Patricia. No one calls me Patricia anymore. I'm sorry, Magnolia. It makes me feel better to laugh at things. If I didn't laugh, I'd cry. I shouldn't make fun of your name. When I was younger, people used to taunt me over my name. Pattie, Pattie is a fattie. I won't tell you the rest."

"You're not fat at all."

"Well, for years I was convinced I was. I still feel fat and ugly."

Magnolia's heart softened when she saw tears brim in Pattie's eyes. She thought hard what to say to comfort her. "You're a very attractive girl, Pattie, and don't ever let yourself think otherwise, okay?"

Pattie nodded.

"And, I'm sorry all this has happened to you, with the fire and everything, but *Gott* sometimes makes good things come from bad situations."

*"Jah,* that's what Benjamin keeps saying." Pattie's head was still lowered and she didn't look cheered up one little bit. Magnolia looked at the dress Pattie was wearing. It was far too big for her petite frame. "Why don't I buy you some fabric and have Mary Lou make you a lovely dress, and a new cape, *kapp* and apron. My treat."

"Oh, Magnolia. I couldn't let you do that."

"You certainly could! I want to. It would make me happy. You'd be doing me a favor."

Pattie sniffed. "Would Mary Lou mind?"

"She was the one who suggested it." Magnolia knew Mary Lou would love to do it. Besides, maybe she had suggested it. Half the time Magnolia didn't listen when Mary Lou talked to her. "She would've come here herself, but it's not easy to get away with three young *kinner.* There's always one that's down for a nap, and the little one is constantly feeding."

"Still, I couldn't."

"You can and you will. Just as soon as we finish this." She lifted her mug. "I insist. Did you have anything better to do today?"

"I don't know what Zach's got planned."

"Okay, if he says he doesn't mind and if you have nothing planned, shall we do it?"

*"Jah, denke,* Magnolia. And, I'm really sorry for calling you a magpie."

"Don't worry, I've been called much worse."

Pattie laughed and so did Magnolia.

## CHAPTER 14

WHEN THEY WERE FINISHED with their coffee, they put their coats on and went outside to find Zach. They gave up after several minutes of looking and calling out.

"He's gone for a long walk, I guess," Pattie said.

"He can't have plans. Why don't you leave him a note?"

*"Nee,* he'll figure out I've gone somewhere. Besides, he might not be back until after we return."

"Okay, well, let's go." They climbed up into the buggy. "First we'll have to stop by Mary Lou's and she can figure out how much fabric we'll need. I suppose I should have her give me some lessons. I can sew okay, but she's better than anyone I know. She could make a good living out of it."

"Okay. I'm in your hands. Make me look as pretty as you."

Magnolia smiled at Pattie and found she was beginning to like her a little more.

To Magnolia's relief, Mary Lou didn't look at all surprised when she turned up at the house with Pattie. She measured Pattie with her dressmaker's tape and wrote down what types of fabrics to get and how many yards to buy of each.

"So, what do you think of Zach?" Pattie asked Magnolia as they made their way to town in the buggy.

Had she guessed she liked Zach? Magnolia glanced over at her. "What do you mean?"

"You asked me about him and earlier he asked me about you. Something's going on." Pattie wiggled her eyebrows.

Magnolia couldn't stop a smile from tugging at the corners of her mouth. "Really? He asked you about me?"

*"Jah."*

"What did he say?"

"Just asked this and that. I can't give too much away."

Magnolia giggled. "Come on. Just tell me."

"It was nothing much. Just how long you were staying and what I know about you."

That wiped the smile off Magnolia's face. "I hope he hasn't heard anything bad about me."

"Don't be silly. What could possibly be bad?"

Magnolia fixed her eyes back on the road. "Nothing."

~

IT WAS the next day when Mary Lou had just got the baby to sleep and had settled down with Magnolia to start sewing the dress for Pattie when there was a loud knock on the door. Mary Lou jumped up from the table to answer it. When she swung the door open, she was surprised to see two large uniformed policemen.

"Can I help you?"

"Good morning. This is Constable Reynolds, and I'm Constable Hart. We're hoping we might be able to ask you some questions regarding the fire at the house of Pattie Reid."

She gulped. "Why are you asking me?"

"We're asking everyone who knows the Reids and all those who live nearby."

"Oh, yes. Come in." Rather than take them to the kitchen where the fabric pieces were cut out, she took them to the living room where they sat down.

They asked her a range of questions including how well she knew Pattie Reid. Mary Lou hoped that Jacob wouldn't be angry with her for letting them into the house.

"Have you gotten any closer to finding out who did it?"

"We're questioning as many people as we can."

Mary Lou looked expectantly from one officer to the other. That hadn't answered her question, but they probably weren't allowed to tell her anything.

"You don't know of any enemies the Reids had?"

"No, I don't. And it was just Pattie living there now that her brother had moved away. He's back here now."

"He's come back now, you say?"

"That's right." Mary Lou noticed the officers exchanged glances. "You're not thinking Pattie did it to make her brother come back?"

"Why? Is that what you think?" Officer Hart asked with his pen poised.

"No, she wouldn't do such a thing. That was her home." Still nervous at what Jacob would say about the police, she stood up. "I think I've answered enough questions."

Magnolia made a noise from the kitchen sounding like she'd dropped the scissors, maybe. Constable Reynolds cocked his head. "Perhaps there's someone else here we should question?"

"I'm here with my three children, who are having a nap, and my cousin. My cousin has nothing to say."

The officers stood, thanked her for her time and headed out the door.

Once they were gone, Mary Lou felt a whole lot better.

Magnolia stuck her head around the kitchen doorway. "They've gone?"

"*Jah.* Did you hear what they said?"

"I did. Why would they want to question me?"

Magnolia had said that in such a way it made Mary Lou think harder. She'd told Magnolia about Zach and how nice he was. What if she burned down the house trying to have him return? Magnolia had stated before that she wasn't too keen on an older man or a widower. Would she go to those lengths? Given what she'd done with Samuel's letters to and from Catherine during her last visit, Mary Lou was afraid she might go to the lengths of burning down a house. She had seemed totally unrepentant about those letters. Was it possible that burning down a house was the next step in Magnolia's madness?

"Well, Mary Lou?"

"Oh, I don't know. They heard a noise in the kitchen and wondered if they should question you. Then I asked them to leave. Perhaps I shouldn't have talked to them at all."

"Yeah, I wouldn't have let them in."

"Well, it's too late now. They said they're talking to everyone. I wonder who did it. They said it was deliberately lit."

"I don't know. Do you want to keep working on this dress before Jimmy wakes?"

Mary Lou shrugged off her worry. "*Jah,* let's do it."

# CHAPTER 15

It was the Saturday of the horse race and Jacob and Zach had decided between them to travel in Zach's buggy, as it could fit more people.

Ivy was looking after Mary Lou's oldest two and only the baby was going with them. While the baby stayed asleep in the buggy, Magnolia got out and helped Mary Lou into Ivy's house with Adam and Lucinda. Before they got to the door, Zach opened it.

"Who do we have here?"

Magnolia had Lucinda in her arms. "This is Lucinda, the middle one. That's Adam, and baby Jimmy's asleep in the buggy." She could sense Mary Lou staring at her and she laughed. "Oh, sorry, Mary Lou. I should've let you say who everyone was."

"It's okay, I'm sure Zach knows they're mine."

"I know Lucinda and Adam and I know about Jimmy, but I haven't met him yet." He opened the door for them to get through. "I'll wait in the buggy with Jacob."

When Magnolia placed Lucinda on the floor of the living room, she whispered to Mary Lou. "Do you think he likes me?"

"He certainly gave you a big smile. And I'm sure he meant just for you to go with him today. I feel dreadful about the confusion."

"Don't worry, it's not your fault," Magnolia said.

"Here they are."

Both girls turned to see Mrs. Fuller coming out of the kitchen. Adam grabbed Mary Lou's skirt and hung on.

"Oh, he knows you're going, Mary Lou."

"They'll be all right. If they start to cry, just keep going," Mrs. Fuller said.

"Distract them with cookies," Magnolia suggested as Mary Lou tried to open Adam's hand to get her dress back.

Mrs. Fuller chortled. "I know all the *grossmammi* tricks." She picked up Adam, and he squealed.

"Run for it, Mary Lou." Magnolia pulled on Mary Lou's sleeve.

Mary Lou's eyes widened and she looked down at Lucinda, whose bottom lip was wobbling. "I can't go."

*"Jah,* you can. Go now." Mrs. Fuller held Adam on her hip and with the other hand, she held on to Lucinda's hand. "Trust me, they settle as soon as you're gone."

"And, I'm not going by myself," Magnolia hissed in her ear. "Not now."

"Okay, I'm going."

Once they were back in the buggy, and on their way, Magnolia gave a sigh of relief.

"I was just telling Jacob that these races are only small. Not like the ones in Unionville," Zach said.

Magnolia nodded. "I figured that, but it'll still be good to see them. The last time I went to a horse race was when I was about eight. A friend of my father's owned a racing horse, if my memory serves me right."

Magnolia and Zach talked away in the front seat of the buggy until they arrived at the racetrack.

Once they were there, Mary Lou cleverly steered Jacob in a different direction and Zach and Magnolia were left on their own.

"I'm glad you could make it here today." Zach smiled at Magnolia.

"Me too. I think we'll have a good time."

"I wanted it to be just us, but I shouldn't have asked you in front of Jacob. He got the wrong idea. Would you have come if it were just me and you?"

"*Jah,* that would have been much better."

He smiled and looked down at the ground as they walked. "Maybe we could do something else, just the two of us? Sometime soon?"

"Okay." Magnolia knew there was no mistake this time. This was a definite date.

They sat together and watched races while Zach

explained everything to her, about the horses and the rigs. She found out that the friend he worked for designed the racing rigs and had them made. It was lunchtime in one of the refreshments tents when they met up with a tired-looking Mary Lou and Jacob again.

After they ate, Jacob said, "I'll take Mary Lou home and come back for you."

"*Nee,* we can find our own way home," Zach said.

Magnolia looked at Mary Lou and knew she'd done a good job. She must've told Jacob what was going on. "You do look exhausted, Mary Lou."

"I am." She looked down at Jimmy, who was in Jacob's arms. "Jimmy can sleep anywhere he wants."

"You two take my buggy and go. Don't worry about us. I'll have Magnolia home safe and sound before dark."

*This day couldn't be working out any better,* thought Magnolia.

# CHAPTER 16

BENJAMIN HAD plans in his own mind that Pattie might agree to go on a date. He waited until his mother was busy with Mary Lou and Jacob's children. Pattie was shelling peas in the kitchen and Jacob sat down next to her.

"How about you and I do something together?" He picked up a couple of peas and popped them into his mouth.

"Okay, like what?"

He was delighted she agreed so quickly. "What would you like to do?"

"Wait a minute. Are you talking like a date or something?"

*"Jah.* Exactly like that."

She shook her head and resumed shelling the peas. *"Nee,* I can't do that."

"Why not?"

"Because you dated two of my cousins. I told you that. Georgia and Marlene."

*"Jah,* I remember them, but are you sure her name was Marlene?"

She nodded.

"Hmm, I suppose you would know, being her cousin and all."

"I'm truly grateful for all you've done, Benjamin, and we can be friends."

Benjamin nodded and tried to hide his disappointment. "'Friends is good. Friends are better than enemies." He stood up. He wasn't going to hang around there all day and do nothing. They were waiting on another delivery of timber on Monday before more work could be done on her house.

"Benjamin, I want to do something nice for your parents for having me stay here. Mostly for your *Mamm.* Can you think of anything?"

*"Nee.* I can't."

"What does she like?"

"Cooking, cleaning, the usual things."

"Really? Or does she just do those things because she has to?"

Benjamin scratched the back of his neck. He never thought too much about it. "I can't say."

"Oh, well, I'll have to think of something by myself."

"Okay." He took a step toward the door and turned back. "Will you go on a date with me?"

*"Nee."*

"This is your last chance?"

*"Nee."*

He took two more steps, stopped and turned around to face her. "I'm really going this time."

*"Nee,* Benjamin." She giggled and threw a pea pod at him.

He smiled, scooped down and picked it up. His mother would be horrified if she knew Pattie was throwing food. "I'll see you tonight then." He gave her a wink, popped the whole peapod in his mouth, turned and headed outside to hitch his buggy.

BENJAMIN NEEDED SOME OLDER-BROTHER ADVICE, and was pleased to find Isaac at home oiling his harnesses in the barn.

"You see, no woman has ever refused me when I asked them on a date. What does she see that's wrong with me?" He put his arms out and turned in a full circle.

Isaac stifled a laugh. "Did you ask her?"

Benjamin sat down on the edge of a hay bale. *"Nee.* I can't ask her because that would be weird."

Isaac scratched his forehead with his arm since his hands were covered in oil. "The moment's passed anyway, I suppose."

"Well, what should I do?"

"Nothing, she said no. What more can you do?"

"That's what I'm asking you." Benjamin shook his head. "I don't know if I'm asking the right person."

"I'm sorry, but I don't know what you want me to say."

"That's okay. Don't worry about it." Benjamin realized he should be talking to Timothy. He'd gone through a rough time with Taylor and now they were happily married. "I'll talk to Timothy."

"That might be best. I've been married so long I can't remember anything about courting a woman. I hope I never have to go through it again."

"Don't worry, I'll figure it out." Benjamin sighed.

"Why don't you stay for dinner?"

He looked through the double barn doors at the house. One of the children was crying. As much as he loved them, it was a noise he didn't want to be around. Not know, especially. *"Denke,* but I told *Mamm* I'd be back in time for dinner."

"Okay."

"I'll say hello and goodbye to Hazel and her *mudder."*

Benjamin said goodbye to Hazel, her *mudder,* who lived with them, and the *kinner,* and then he headed home. All the way there, he couldn't stop thinking of Pattie.

# CHAPTER 17

AFTER DINNER THAT NIGHT, Pattie was helping Benjamin's mother in the kitchen, and the men had been told to sit in the living room. When Benjamin's father went to the bathroom, Zach started the conversation. "We'll be moving out soon. We've had the clean-up crew in and the frame will go up next weekend."

Benjamin didn't want Pattie to leave the house. He'd barely see her. "You can't expect Pattie to live there until the place is perfect and complete. It'll be a while before that happens."

Zach, who was sitting on the same couch, leaned over and placed his hand on Benjamin's shoulder. "Are you looking for my approval?"

"What do you mean?"

"It's no secret you're in love with her."

Benjamin frowned. "Is it that obvious?"

"It is to me. Have you asked her out?"

*"Jah,* but she refuses me every time."

"Do you want me to have a word with her?"

Benjamin shook his head. *"Denke,* but I don't want her to feel obligated to go out with me."

"Okay, suit yourself."

He reconsidered, figuring he might need a little help. Rubbing his slightly bristly chin, he asked, "What would you say?"

"I'd just tell her I think you'd be a good choice and she should give you a chance."

He thought about that for a moment. "I guess that wouldn't hurt."

"Too late, you already said you didn't need my help."

Benjamin laughed and gave him a playful shove. "You're both hard work, you and your *schweschder."*

"I'll say something tonight when she comes out of the kitchen, when your parents aren't listening. You go to bed early and I'll talk to her. Ask her again in the morning, and she might say yes. I can tell she likes you."

"Hmm. Could've fooled me. And where were you today?"

"I was with Magnolia."

"Magnolia? Mary Lou's cousin, Magnolia?"

Zach's face beamed with delight. *"Jah,* I really like her. We had such a *wunderbaar* time together. She tells me she wants to be a teacher. I admire a woman who likes to work and keep busy."

"She's one-of-a-kind, that's for sure and for certain."

They both stopped talking when Mr. Fuller sat down with them. "What are you two scheming about?"

"We're figuring out when Zach's *haus* will be ready for Pattie to move back into."

Mr. Fuller said, "We got Timothy's up fast a few years ago. There's no reason we can't do the same."

"We're both working at the *haus* tomorrow."

"Very good." Mr. Fuller picked up the Amish paper, unfolded it and began to read.

When the women came out of the kitchen, Benjamin did what Zach had suggested and retired for an early night.

~

IN THE MIDDLE of Sunday night, Benjamin got up to grab a snack. Nervousness had prevented him from eating very much with Pattie sitting opposite. When he reached the bottom of the stairs, he was surprised to see a glow of light coming from the kitchen. He walked in and saw Pattie drinking a mug of something hot. She had her prayer *kapp* on, but he could see her hair was bundled under it in a careless manner, and she wore an oversized dressing gown, most likely one of his mother's.

"Oh, Pattie. You're awake. Have you gone to bed yet?"

"*Jah,* but I couldn't sleep."

"Me either. What have you got there?"

"Chamomile tea. It helps me to sleep. Want one?"

"Okay, I'll try it. Don't get up, just point me in the direction of the tea."

"I use tea bags and they're on the sink."

He walked over, grabbed a mug from the cupboard, added a bag of chamomile, and poured hot water over the teabag. All the while, he wondered if Zach had gotten a chance to talk to Pattie. Was that why she couldn't sleep? Perhaps she was worried about how to let him down gently?

When he sat opposite her, he asked, "Are you worried about something?"

*"Nee,* are you?"

He shook his head and then took a sip of tea.

"I often have trouble sleeping since my parents' died. It still feels odd that they're gone and now Zach's moved away, and I'm alone now. I haven't gotten used to it."

"You'll feel better once your *haus* is finished."

"My *bruder* says I should give you a chance."

He stared at her to judge what she thought about that. "Smart man."

She smiled and looked down into her tea. When she looked up again, she said, "The thing is, I'm not ready yet. Maybe when I'm living back home I will be ready."

He took a mouthful of tea and it scalded his mouth. His face twisted and he wanted to spit it out, but he had to swallow it. He felt it scald his throat on the way down, and hopped up for a swallow of cool water.

"Are you okay?"

"That was hot." He breathed in deeply. "I'll wait."

"For the tea to cool?" she asked.

*"Jah,* that would be smart, and for you to be ready to go out with me."

"I can't ask you to do that."

His lips twisted into a smile. "Are we still talking about the hot tea?"

She giggled. "Wait for me."

"I want to."

"Really? But what—"

*"Nee,* enough said. Don't ruin my day before it begins. I'll wait, and it doesn't matter for how long, and I'm not talking about the tea, okay?"

She covered her mouth with her fingertips and giggled.

He glanced at the clock. "I have to be up in a few hours."

*"Jah,* you're working on the *haus* with Zach."

"This is true, if the timber is delivered. It's supposed to be there at six, so we'll see. It's one of our regular suppliers so they're supposed to be reliable."

"I wanted to go too, but your *mudder* is insisting I stay. I probably would only get in the way over there."

He leaned closer. "One thing I've learned is that things go better if everyone does what my mother wants."

"I kind of figured that out already."

They sat and talked for another half hour before they both decided they should get some sleep.

# CHAPTER 18

THE NEXT MORNING, Pattie woke a little later than usual. She stretched her arms over her head like a lazy cat. Today, she felt different—needed and loved. It had made a difference to her to hear how Benjamin was so attracted to her, and she knew he was. His feelings toward her made her feel she belonged somewhere and she hadn't felt that way since her parents died. Would Benjamin be the man she'd marry? The inner glow inside her and the happiness bubbling within told her he would be. Now, she had to be careful to make a good impression on his mother, and sleeping in was not the thing to do in an Amish household, especially one with a matriarch as strong as Mrs. Fuller.

Pattie jumped out of bed and got dressed, pulling on today's set of the borrowed clothing. It was a dark green dress and she couldn't remember which of the Fuller wives had kindly given it to her. After she had drawn a brush through her long hair, she braided and pinned it up, and then put on a white prayer *kapp.* Next were black stockings and black lace up shoes. Her feet were exactly the same size as Mrs. Fuller's.

Staying at the Fullers' place was nice. There were always people coming and going and many lively conversations were had. It'd be hard to go back to her lonely existence after this.

Next it was into the bathroom to clean her teeth and wash her face, which she did extra quickly before she headed down to the kitchen.

"I'm sorry I'm late, Mrs. Fuller."

"Call me Ivy."

She'd told her that many times before. *"Jah,* Ivy."

"You don't have to be anywhere do you?"

*"Nee,* but I like to wake early enough to help you when you wake up and I'm afraid I slept in today."

Mrs. Fuller glanced at the clock. "No matter. Sit and I'll cook you breakfast."

*"Nee,* I can do it."

"I insist."

Pattie sat, feeling bad that she was causing Mrs. Fuller extra work. "The boys woke early to go to my *haus* today."

*"Ach jah,* they've got half the community over there today. Your *haus* will be up in no time."

"What do you have planned for the day?" Pattie asked.

"Today is washing day and by the looks of it, it should be a *gut* drying day."

"I'll help."

Mrs. Fuller chuckled. "If you want, you can. I'll appreciate the extra hands."

WHEN BREAKFAST WAS OVER, Pattie and Mrs. Fuller went out the back door. Ivy was filling the gas-powered washing machine with linen when they both heard a car approaching the *haus*. They looked at each other and then walked a few steps and looked around the corner of the house to confirm what they heard. A woman was getting out of a parked car.

"Can you go see what they want, Pattie? She would've lost her way. We get a few tourists on this road."

"Okay." Pattie went back through the house and opened the front door to see a pretty young *Englisch* woman in the yard. She was wearing jeans, high-heeled boots and a pink off-the-shoulder blouse. "Hello."

The woman was halfway between the house and the car, and continued to walk toward Pattie. "Hello, is this Benjamin Fuller's house?"

Pattie hoped this wasn't what it looked like. "Yes, it is."

"Is he at home right now?"

"No. He's at work."

Her pink painted nails flew to her matching lips.

"Oh, he said he'd only be here for a short stay. I didn't think he'd be working."

Pattie narrowed her eyes. This woman seemed to know Benjamin pretty well. "You're a friend?"

"Yes. Didn't he mention me?" The girl looked worried and then quickly hid one of her hands behind her back.

Pattie guessed she was hiding a ring. An *Englisch* engagement ring perhaps? "Um, do you want to come inside to wait for him? He's not expected back until nightfall."

"Are you his sister?"

"No."

"I'll wait for him."

Pattie was surprised the woman was going to wait until nightfall because it wasn't yet midday. The woman kept walking toward her and Pattie stepped back and allowed the girl into the house. Then, Pattie pointed to the couch. "Have a seat there and I'll get Benjamin's mother."

"Okay thanks."

She sat down and then Pattie rushed to Mrs. Fuller, who was just outside the kitchen. "Ivy, there's a girl here. She says she's come to see Benjamin."

Mrs. Fuller dried her hands. "An *Englisch* girl?"

*"Jah."*

"What's he done now?"

Pattie shrugged her shoulders. "I'll stay here while you find out."

Mrs. Fuller walked into the house and Pattie sat down at the kitchen table. The conversation that followed between the two women was just what Pattie had feared. Benjamin was engaged to the girl. If he was engaged to this woman, what was he doing asking her out?

One thing she knew was that as soon as she could, she'd go back home. She didn't want to rush out and make a scene. She'd be calm and quiet, and leave that way too.

The next thing she knew, Mrs. Fuller rushed into the kitchen crying into a handkerchief. "Oh, can you talk to her, Pattie?"

"What's wrong?"

Mrs. Fuller shook her head and sat, apparently too upset to speak. Pattie walked into the living room and the girl was just at the door ready to leave. "Oh. I thought you were waiting."

The woman swung around to look at Pattie. "I didn't mean to upset anyone. I didn't know Benjamin was keeping me a secret."

"I'm sure there's a reasonable explanation."

"I'm certain there is and I reckon it's not too hard to figure out what it is." She headed out the door and Pattie followed her.

"Do you want me to tell Benjamin you were here?"

"He knows where to find me." Without turning around, the girl got back in her car and drove away.

Pattie rushed back into the house and sat by Mrs. Fuller. "What did she say?"

"I can't say it."

Pattie didn't know what to do. "Shall I call someone for you?"

She shook her head.

"I heard a little bit of what she said, and figured out the rest. I'll make you a cup of hot tea." Mrs. Fuller didn't respond, so she went ahead and made two cups of tea. When she'd placed the cup of tea in front of Benjamin's mother, she sat next to her. "She said she's engaged to Benjamin?"

Mrs. Fuller nodded. "I hope this isn't a repeat of Timothy and Taylor. I couldn't go through that again. I thought him going away would make a man out of him, a good Amish man, not drive him into the arms of the Devil."

All Pattie wanted to do was go home and cry. Benjamin had deceived her and he wasn't the man for her. She couldn't go home, though. She had no home to go to, and besides, she had to stay and comfort Mrs. Fuller.

# CHAPTER 19

WHEN THEY HEARD the rattling of a wagon, Mrs. Fuller jumped to her feet and rushed to the window. "Here he is now. I can't speak with him."

Pattie stood and realized that they'd decided to come home for the midday meal. "I'll find out what's going on." Pattie felt like a fool. Only this morning she had the idea of marrying Benjamin.

*"Denke."* Mrs. Fuller sat back down.

"There you are." Benjamin said when he saw Pattie walking toward him. "I was hoping you'd still be here."

Zach wasn't with Benjamin. That was good. Now she'd have the chance to speak with him alone. "Your *mudder* and I had a visitor here today. I didn't catch her name, but she was very pretty."

Benjamin dropped the reins he was securing and stared at her. "I can explain."

Pattie crossed her arms over her chest. "Go on."

"I met her in Ohio a year after I left, and … How much did she tell you?"

"She said you were engaged."

"What? *Nee,* I wasn't. We absolutely were not. What else did she say?"

"There's more?"

He looked away. "Forget it."

"Well, your *mudder* is going to ask you what happened."

"This is what happened. She saw me in the street about to get into my buggy, and she asked me if she could get a ride, saying she lived a few streets away. She was pretty and innocent looking, and I didn't see any harm in it. All I did was drive her home and talked to her along the way. She's been tracking me ever since, to every place I've gone. I never told her where I live, here I mean, but it seems she's found out."

"You didn't give her a ring?"

"What? *Nee!"*

"She looked like she was trying to hide a ring."

"I didn't give it to her. That was all an act. I told her more than once there can never be anything between us, that I would never date outside the Amish." He glanced up at the house. "She didn't speak to *Mamm,* did she?"

*"Jah,* she did, and your *mudder* is in the kitchen trying to get her head around it."

*"Ach nee."* He took his hat off and ran a hand through his hair.

"She's upset."

"I'm sure, and I'm sorry. I thought Kylie had given up on chasing me. I never should've given her that ride."

"It seems that being impulsive is something you have a problem with. When you asked me out, were you being impulsive then?" She thought maybe he was far too secretive, too.

*"Nee,* I was totally serious, but I don't blame you for being mad with me."

"I'd leave right now if Ivy wasn't so upset. Go on inside. You'd better tell her your story."

He stepped closer. "It's not a story, it's the truth."

"It no longer matters to me. I'll wait on the porch." Pattie turned away from him as she held back tears, and walked back to the house and he followed close behind. She'd feel much better if she could run away, back to the safety of her home.

WHEN MR. FULLER arrived home ten minutes later, Pattie saw her opportunity to leave. Benjamin still hadn't come out of the house and she heard him consoling his mother. "Hello, Mr. Fuller. I was just leaving. Do you mind saying goodbye to Ivy for me, and tell her I'll be back in a few hours?"

"Certainly, but what's happened that you can't say goodbye yourself?"

"Um, she's having quite a serious conversation

with Benjamin and I didn't want to interrupt." Before he could ask another thing, she asked to borrow one of his buggies, so she could check on the building progress of her home. When he agreed, she wasted no time in hitching the buggy to Chester, her horse, and jumped into it. When she was halfway down the driveway, she glanced in the rear-view mirror at the house. Liking Benjamin had been stupid. It was another disappointment, but it could've been worse. She turned onto the road, determined to put love, romance, and such things, out of her mind.

~

BENJAMIN LOOKED up and saw his father coming in the front door. "*Dat,* come and sit with us."

"You won't believe what's happened now," Ivy said to her husband.

"*Mamm,* please let me explain it."

Ten minutes and a lot of explaining later, Mr. Fuller rubbed his beard. "Why was this girl so fixated on you?"

"It must be my charm and charisma." When Benjamin saw his jokes weren't lightening the mood, he said, "Okay, I'm sorry for saying that. I thought she was gone, and this was a thing I wasn't going to tell you because I didn't want to worry you. When I got to her place, her ex-boyfriend was there and he threatened her. I told him to stop and he ended up leaving. I guess she was grateful, or something."

"She saw you as her hero," his mother said.

"Maybe," Benjamin said, glad his mother was finally making sense out of the whole thing. "But, we never even had a relationship. All I did was give a stranger a ride home, and I talked to her ex-boyfriend."

"An *Englischer,* Benjamin. That's why the Word says not to mix with the people of the world."

"I didn't see the harm in giving her a ride."

His mother lifted her chin. "Do you see the harm now?"

*"Jah,* absolutely, I do now. They can't all be the same, though. I've met some wonderful people who aren't Amish."

Mr. Fuller grunted. "When are you coming back to work, son?"

"I'll talk to Isaac about it. In a week or two I think. I just want to make sure Zach and Pattie's house is well underway."

"It's not your responsibility to oversee the *haus.* There are a team of men from the community who've taken control of it."

"I know, but I care about the two of them."

Mrs. Fuller smiled. "You're a *gut bu."*

Benjamin chuckled. He felt about five years old when his mother said that.

"We've got a lot of work going on in the shop. The boys could use your help."

Benjamin knew his father wanted him to return to work at the family's shop because he thought it would keep him out of trouble. "Okay, I'll start soon. I'll talk to Isaac next time I see him."

His father gave a sharp nod. "See that you do."

"So, are we all good now?"

"That poor girl seems to think you're engaged to her."

"I can't help what she thinks, *Mamm.* Everything I told you is true."

His father nodded. "We believe you."

Benjamin was relieved. Everything he told them was true, but there were some other things he'd held back, things he knew they wouldn't want to know.

## CHAPTER 20

WHILE MAGNOLIA WAS off helping at school again, Mary Lou visited her *schweschder*-in-law, Catherine. Their children were quietly playing together and Mary Lou's baby was asleep in her arms. Mary Lou took a deep breath, and raised her suspicions. "Catherine, do you think Magnolia could've started the fire?"

"The fire at the Reids' house?"

*"Jah."*

"What would make you think that?"

The children had just finished milk and cookies and now it was the adult's turn to have something. Catherine joined Mary Lou at the kitchen table with two mugs of *kaffe* and some ginger and walnut cookies.

Mary Lou took a cookie off the plate. "I told her about Zach and told her he was handsome and single, and then I remembered he'd already left. Magnolia seemed interested in him and then she seemed positive he'd come back home. Then, I said it would take a real emergency to get him to come back."

"Oh, an emergency like a fire, you mean?"

*"Jah,* I know I'm thinking the worst. Do you think she'd be capable of something like that?" Mary Lou took a bite of the cookie.

"Is that the only reason you think she did it?"

Mary Lou shook her head. *"Nee,* there were dirty boots at the door in the morning, and they weren't there the night before. They were definitely Magnolia's. I remember because I was the last one to go to sleep the night before. I fed Jimmy in the middle of the night and went down to get a glass of water. I thought I heard a noise and opened the back door. There was nothing there that I could see, and there were definitely no boots there."

"Did you ask her about it?"

*"Nee,* I didn't think much of it then, and later, after we all learned of the fire, I couldn't."

Catherine leaned back in her chair and brought the coffee mug to her lips and took a sip. "She did a very weird thing with those letters, but that was years ago. You know, when she pretended letters were from me, or from Samuel, when she'd written them. That wasn't dangerous, just selfish."

*"Jah,* but has she changed just because she's older? I tell you she's desperate to marry." Mary Lou took another bite of the cookie. Ginger and walnut were a

strange combination to her, and she wasn't sure whether the flavors fit together.

Catherine placed her mug down on the table, keeping her hands around the warmth of the mug. "She wouldn't kill, though, I'm sure, and fires are so dangerous."

"I don't know."

"You really think she did it?" Catherine searched Mary Lou's face.

"I think it's a very real possibility. And, I hate to even think that. I mean, what do I do now? Do I confront her with my suspicions? If I did and she hadn't done it, she'd hate me forever."

Catherine shook her head. "It's a hard one. I'm not certain what you should do. If you do nothing, what if she is guilty and she does it again?"

*"Ach nee,* don't say that. She's staying in my *haus,* too."

"Why not say something about the boots?"

"I can't. Too many days have passed. She is getting along with him so well."

"Zach?"

*"Jah,* but she couldn't have known she would've."

"I know. Where is she today?"

"She's spending time with Celia. She's always at the school helping with the students in the morning and then she watches Zach work on his *haus* in the afternoons."

"Hasn't Celia stopped working yet?"

"She'll stop as soon as her replacement gets here, but the new teacher has been delayed."

"I'm sure Magnolia wouldn't have done it."

Mary Lou nodded, and hoped Catherine was right.

MAGNOLIA HAD another good time at the school, helping the children and talking with Celia in the break-time. She stopped her buggy a distance away from Zach's house and went to find him. There were at least twenty men working there, climbing like ants over the roof frame.

When she saw him, he was hammering something that looked like a doorframe, and she hurried over. "Zach."

He looked over his shoulder and, instead of a beaming smile he scowled.

"What's up? Why do you look so grumpy?"

"There's a rumor you set my *haus* alight."

There was a lot of hammering going on, but she couldn't mistake what he'd just said. "Me?"

He nodded.

"Well, that's just ridiculous. Did someone say it was me who did it?"

"It's gossip, but in my experience rumors and gossip have some truth to them." He placed the hammer down on the newly built porch, and placed his hands on his hips. His eyes, once full of softness, were now cruel and cold. "Where there's smoke there's fire."

"This rumor has zero truth to it. You surely can't believe it."

"Why would it come about if it didn't have truth?"

Magnolia swallowed hard. It was the things she'd done in the past come back to bite her. There was no point staying there trying to talk him out of his views. She turned and walked away.

When she reached the buggy, the tears were running down her face. She wiped them away with the back of her hand. She trotted the buggy away, and when she was clear of the house, she walked the buggy. Not wanting to go home and face Mary Lou, she walked the horse back to the schoolhouse. Celia might be able to console her and give her some good advice.

# CHAPTER 21

WHEN MAGNOLIA PULLED up at the schoolhouse, the last of the children were leaving. She secured the horse and walked through the door. Celia was sitting behind her desk going through some papers.

"Magnolia, you're back?"

Magnolia nodded. "Something bad has just happened." Celia already knew all about her feelings for Zach. "I finally thought I had found the man of my dreams, but he accused me of burning down his *haus*. I have no idea why he would think that." Magnolia pulled up a small chair to the desk and sat down.

"He really thinks you did it?"

"I'm pretty sure he does. I mean, he said he heard that I did it. And he believes that rumors contain truth."

"A few years ago I was in nearly the same position."

"Somebody thought you burned down a *haus* too?"

Celia shook her head. "Not quite. I was always

unlucky in love. And then I decided to devote my life to teaching, and I was happy for a few years. And then I met Gabe, and I became even happier."

Magnolia stared at her; head tilted quizzically, and wondered how the little story was meant to comfort her.

"Magnolia, I just received word my replacement's not coming."

"You said she was just late."

"She was late, that's true, but now she's changed her mind."

"That's too bad. You'll have to work right up until the baby comes."

"I'm just getting too tired to do that. It hasn't been easy doing everything. What if you put in for the teacher's job? I will put a good word in for you with the board since you've done a great job so far and all the children like you."

"You mean me become the teacher?"

"Yeah, why not?"

"I don't live here. I'd have to find a permanent place to live."

"You could board with someone for a while until you find yourself a place."

"Do you really think I could do it?" Magnolia's fingertips flew to her lips.

Celia nodded. "I do. You've basically been doing it already, and I can help you all I can. They just can't find a suitable woman to take the job. They advertised it in all the Amish papers, and only the girl from Reading applied."

"My life could be filled with teaching children." Magnolia looked awestruck.

*"Jah,* that's right, and it's very rewarding. It changed my life."

Magnolia giggled. "A few minutes ago, I was sure I'd never laugh again."

"Oh, Magnolia, don't say that. You'll love again, too."

*"Nee,* I'm a lost cause. Even when I'm not doing anything people accuse me of things. Now they've rebuilt the *haus,* I might burn it down again."

Celia gasped. "Don't say things like that, Magnolia, not even as a joke. Someone might overhear you and think you really did it."

Magnolia frowned. "When do you think I'll find out whether I've got the job?"

Celia bundled up the papers she'd been working on and stood up. "I'll drive to Les Yoder's place right now and talk with him. He's the one in charge. The others generally go along with whatever he says. I'll push them for an answer by tomorrow."

*"Denke,* Celia, from the bottom of my heart. This will give my life meaning and purpose. I will be the best teacher ever, just like my old teacher, Miss Shwetz."

"I'll tell you what. Why don't I collect you at six from Mary Lou's? I'll talk to Les now and suggest an emergency meeting of the board. That way, we'll both know tonight."

Magnolia sprang to her feet and clapped her hands with delight.

MAGNOLIA RUSHED BACK to Mary Lou's house to tell her the news. When she burst through the front door, she found Mary Lou sitting on the couch feeding Jimmy, while the two toddlers played by her feet.

Magnolia ruffled Adam's hair and scooped Lucinda into her arms and sat down next to Mary Lou. "Good news! A teacher position has come available. Celia can't do it for much longer with the *boppli* coming and all. Her replacement has cancelled and now the school really need a teacher. They're desperate. She asked me if I'd like to be the new teacher."

"She asked you? Just like that?"

Lucinda squirmed out of her arms, and Magnolia put her back on the floor. "*Jah,* she did."

"I didn't even know that would be an option."

"It is. I mentioned I was thinking about being a teacher, and I asked her how to become one. I never thought I'd be able to do it. I mean, I knew I could. I was very good in school and always at the top of the class."

"I'm so happy for you, Magnolia. You're so good with children. I can see this working out really well."

"Would you mind if I stay here, Mary Lou, for a while longer?"

Mary Lou smiled, but she didn't look too happy. "That will be fine. You're always welcome here."

"I'll just stay until I find a permanent home. I don't want to be under your feet forever. This is *wunderbaar* and do you know why?"

*"Nee."*

"I don't need to be married now. I'll devote myself to my students just like Miss Shwetz."

"Who's Miss Shwetz?"

"Was. She died. She was my teacher and she was the nicest person there ever was and the best teacher anyone ever had. I want to be just like her."

"And you will be. You can still marry, though."

Magnolia didn't even want to think about Zach. It was too painful to bring to mind his cold eyes. "I need to give that idea up. If *Gott* wanted me to marry, He would've found me someone by now. *Nee, Gott* has other plans and now He's revealed them to me at long last. Now, I just need to be approved by the school board. Like I said, they're desperate and I have Celia on my side, too."

"You'll be fine, especially with her recommendation."

"They have an emergency meeting tonight and Celia's going to put my name forward. She's picking me up at six."

"Six tonight? You're going?"

"*Jah.* See? Celia's become a real friend, not a fake one."

"We better hurry up with dinner so you can eat before you go." Mary Lou looked down at Magnolia's clothes. "And borrow something of mine."

"*Denke* I will." Magnolia put her hand over her tummy. "I'll help you with the meal, but I'm too nervous to eat. I'll eat when I come home."

"I'll keep it in the oven for you."

"This is life-changing."

"I know, but how will your folks feel about you moving here?"

"They'll be fine. They can come visit when *Dat* gets better."

Mary Lou tipped her head to one side. "What's wrong with him? I thought he was better."

"He had an accident with a plough." He was always laid up with one thing after another. It was a good thing he shared the farm and the proceeds thereof with his two cousins.

"Oh no. I didn't know."

"He's very accident prone."

"It seems like it."

Magnolia giggled. "Will you pray for me, Mary Lou? Pray I'll get the teaching job? Then I'll be able to save up and get my own place, or find someone who'll take in a boarder. I know you don't have enough room here."

MARY LOU SMILED and gave a little nod in agreement. She'd have to have a private word with Jacob to postpone their house extension. "If you get this job, a nice place to live will also fall into your lap. *Gott* is watching over you."

"I finally feel like He is. That's why it didn't work out with all those men. *Gott* wanted me to be just like Miss Shwetz. Oh, what if the board ask me difficult questions?"

"Just tell them you're here to stay. You're living with me until you find a more permanent place, and you're willing to stay for years. They just want someone stable. It also might help that you're unmarried."

*"Jah,* that's what I thought too. Especially since they've just lost Celia because she got pregnant."

As they peeled the vegetables together, Mary Lou wondered whether Magnolia would be as happy and fulfilled in her new role as she thought she'd be. She was excited about it now, but would that last?

"Zach and I had a fight."

Mary Lou was surprised. They'd been getting along so well. Now she knew why Magnolia was so excited about the teaching job. "What about?"

"There's a rumor going around that I started the fire at his *haus."*

"Oh, how awful." Mary Lou felt bad and looked hard at Magnolia to see if her cousin knew anything, if someone might have mentioned she'd said something.

Catherine must've mentioned something to her husband, who then mentioned it to someone else.

"I can't believe he'd think such a thing."

"What did he say exactly?" Mary Lou asked.

"Nothing much, he just asked me if I did it and said there was a rumor. He didn't say who said it. I'd like to find out."

Mary Lou shrugged her shoulders. "Who knows how these things get started?"

"How could he think I would do such a thing?"

"I don't know. So, things are over between the two of you?"

"Over. Completely over before anything really began. I could never feel the same way about him. Besides, I'm pretty sure he's got a temper. He throws things."

Mary Lou felt awful now for voicing her concerns to Catherine. This would teach her a good lesson, to keep her mouth shut in the future. She couldn't ask Magnolia about those dusty boots she'd seen by the door that morning, not now.

At the meeting of the board at Les Yoder's house, Magnolia was the most nervous she'd ever been in her life.

Celia told them how she'd helped her, and how the children had taken to her. Then and there the board offered her the job. And, to Magnolia's surprise, the pay was more than she had expected. On that wage, she could make a life for herself as a single woman just like Miss Shwetz had done. There'd be no time to go home to visit her parents, so she'd call them or maybe write, and she could go back home during the next school break and collect her belongings at the same time. This was the beginning of a new life for Magnolia, and she was determined to make the most of it.

## CHAPTER 22

BENJAMIN WAITED for the next opportunity to talk with Pattie alone. It came at midnight in the kitchen when they both couldn't sleep, once again.

"Are you totally fine now I've explained everything about Kylie?"

*"Jah.* I guess so."

"Now we've got that cleared up, why have you been so reluctant to go anywhere with me?"

She figured she'd tell him the truth since he'd told her about Kylie. "You were one of the boys at school who taunted me."

He was sick to the stomach. *"Nee,* I never was. I know the boys who did, and they weren't me. I wasn't part of it."

"Are you certain it wasn't you?"

"I'm certain. I can remember them doing it. They

were younger boys. Older than you, but younger than me."

"Oh! I remember now, that's right."

He shook his head. "I'm sorry it happened to you. It was awful. There's no excuse for that kind of thing. It's a wonder you've ever talked to me again if you thought I was one of those boys."

"I never told anyone how much it upset me. Not even my *bruder.*"

"You're not a fattie, you're just right, and you have a beautiful face, and that was true back then, too."

"You do remember."

He nodded. "I do. Those things aren't tolerated in the community."

"I know. They stopped after a while. I'm glad it wasn't you. It was one of the Sanderson boys who was the ringleader, I think."

He smiled. "And I'm glad you've finally realized I had nothing at all to do with it."

"I'm over it now, I think, but it hurt me for a long time. It was humiliating. I think that's why I've always kept to myself."

"You must let it go. It was years ago, and those people are probably ashamed they said those things now they've grown up."

"I guess. I'd like to think they're sorry."

"Why don't I drive you over to your *haus* tomorrow morning so I can show you what progress we've made?"

"I've heard we've got a heavy snowfall headed this way tomorrow."

"They're always saying that this time of year. If the weather's fine, will you come with me?"

"Sure."

~

BENJAMIN HAD MANAGED to bring Pattie to see the house even though the sky was growing dark.

The house was at lock-up stage. The roof, doors and windows, and walls were all up. The fireplace was the only thing that had survived the fire, apart from some parts of walls that had needed to be removed because they were smoke-permeated.

Soon after they stepped inside the house, the wind whipped up and the forecasted snowfall came. Benjamin was pleased he'd thought to put the horse and buggy in the barn.

"Looks like we're not going anywhere for a while," he said.

"What do you mean? We can't stay here alone together."

"We're not going anywhere in this storm."

"I told you the sky looked weird."

"I just wanted to show you the *haus.* Looks like you were right, but still, we can't leave in this." He sat down on the floor and she sat next to him.

"Did you plan this, Benjamin?"

"The weather?"

She nodded. "You probably would've if you could've."

"Wait there." He ran into the barn through the snow and grabbed an armful of firewood, then did the same a few more times.

Pattie watched him load up the firewood by the fireplace, standing with her hands on her hips. "This is just the worst thing that could ever happen."

He stood up and smiled. "Why do you hate me so much?"

"Because you made me like you and then you disappointed me."

He chuckled. "You liked me? Wait, I disappointed you?"

"Once, but not anymore. I don't like to be deceived. I've been thinking more about the girl who came to your place. She was pretty convincing. I can't work out why she'd lie. You must've been lying."

"If you listen to what happened it's a perfectly reasonable explanation. I guess it's not reasonable, but it is an explanation."

"Save your stories. I'm not interested."

He turned away, grabbed some kindling, and lit a fire with a lighter he'd found in his buggy. "Sit by the fire to keep warm. I hope you have food." He took off his wet coat.

*"Nee,* of course not. There's no kitchen yet. Not even a sink."

"No matter."

"Won't your parents worry if we're not back soon with this storm?"

*"Nee,* they know you're with me and I'm a grown man. They'll figure out we're taking shelter somewhere. It doesn't take a genius. Can I tell you what happened now with that girl, Kylie? I'll tell you the full story."

She rolled her eyes. "I knew there was a whole lot more to the story. Go on."

"It was a few years ago now."

"This will be entertaining."

"I can't tell you, if you keep interrupting me."

"Go on." She sat cross-legged beside him.

"It was a few years ago now, as you know, and she had an ex-boyfriend who was troubling her."

"Not the old, *you had to pretend you were her boyfriend to scare off the ex-boyfriend,* story?"

He shook his head.

"Good, because there better be more to it than that."

Benjamin frowned at her. "Do you want to tell the story, or shall I?"

"Go on. I'll keep quiet."

"We got to talking when I was in one of the main streets in town, and she asked if I would take her home in the buggy. She was an attractive girl, so I didn't see the harm in it."

"Of course not, and if she'd been ugly?"

Benjamin chuckled. "She lived only five or ten

minutes away as it turned out. When I arrived, her boyfriend, or ex-boyfriend, or whoever he was, was waiting there pacing up and down by the front door. He shouted at her and yelled in a jealous rage and she called out to him that she should go join the Amish and marry me. It suddenly seemed like she believed her own lies. He yelled at me to step out of the buggy and when I did, he ran at me and swung a punch. I ducked out of the way, and he fell and hit the side of his face on one of the wheel covers of the buggy. He got a nasty gash in his head."

"Really?"

"*Jah.* Then, after swinging another few punches that didn't land, he got in his car and sped off. She asked for my number and address and I stupidly gave her the number where I was staying at the time. Since then, she's been following me around the place, turning up here and there. I guess someone gave her my address here."

"So, she's obsessed with you?"

Benjamin shrugged. "It seems like it."

"Do you often have this trouble with women?"

"That's the only problem I've ever had like that, if that answers your question."

Pattie pouted. "Is that what you told your *mudder?"*

"It's what I told both my parents because it's the truth."

"You never went out with her?"

"That's right." Benjamin shook his head. "I don't know why trouble always follows me."

Without saying anything, Pattie stood and walked up and down rubbing her arms.

"Can you do something about the fire? I'm freezing."

"Sure." He leaped to his feet and started loading more logs onto the fire.

She peeked out the window. "It doesn't look like the snow's letting up."

"Just as well we built your house solidly."

"I don't think the old one would've stood up to the storm. I do appreciate everyone giving up their time to work on the *haus*. I just wish Zach would stay on. He might have done so if things had worked out between him and Magnolia."

"I heard they had a hiccup."

HOURS LATER, the storm had passed and Benjamin was shovelling the snow away from the door and wondering how long before he could use the buggy. They sat and talked for a little longer, and then Benjamin decided they should drive home.

When they got there, they were surprised to see two police cars with lights flashing parked at his house. "What now?" he asked.

"What's happened?" Pattie asked.

He stopped the buggy. "We'll soon find out."

Two officers approached him. "Benjamin Fuller?"

"Yes."

They grabbed him and slapped handcuffs on him. "You're under arrest."

## CHAPTER 23

BENJAMIN SAT in the police interview room trying to drink a mug of the worst coffee he'd ever tasted as Officer Hart and Constable Reynolds asked him the same questions over and over.

"I'm a volunteer firefighter. I didn't start the fire."

"Very often arsonists volunteer as firefighters, and some have been known to start fires."

"That's ridiculous. I was fast asleep when I got the call about the Reids' house."

"And that was right after you enrolled as a volunteer?"

He nodded.

"Convenient."

"Look, those other charges against me were dropped."

"No one bothered to post your bail."

"No one knew. I didn't want anyone to know. It would've killed my mother. She's delicate."

"How did your fingerprints get all over the Reids' barn?"

"I keep telling you, Pattie was staying with us and I went back to get her horses the very next day, the day of the morning of the fire. Pattie wanted to get her horses and bring them to my place because she was afraid they might be stolen. Of course, my fingerprints would be there. I also went back another time to clean out the horses' stalls. I saw the fingerprint team there on my way out. Are mine the only fingerprints you found?"

"Give us a minute." The two officers looked at each other, stood, and walked out of the interview room.

Benjamin had hoped his past would never come back to haunt him. Now his mother would probably find out he'd had a cousin lie for him. While he'd been in prison for the year, he'd sent letters to his cousin who had forwarded them onto his mother. That way, they wouldn't be postmarked as coming from a prison. They'd be postmarked from his cousin's house in Iowa where he had pretended to stay for a whole year.

Ten minutes later, they came back in and sat down. Officer Hart said, "Do you know a Stephen Wallace?"

"No, I don't think so. Should I?"

"Apparently your girlfriend does and he had a grudge against her."

"Girlfriend? You mean Pattie? You think he burned down her house?"

"You're free to go for the moment." Both officers stood.

"Wait a minute, do you have this guy?"

"We have him in custody."

Then he realized they had the other guy's fingerprints too. Benjamin was more than a little relieved.

On his way out of the station, Pattie rushed over to him. "Are you free?"

"Yeah, for now, they said. *Mamm* and *Dat* know I was arrested?"

*"Jah."*

*"Denke* for coming here. They are letting me go and they've arrested someone called Stephen Wallace."

"I know. They asked me about him. The other officers at the *haus* asked me about him. They drove me here so I could wait for you."

Benjamin looked around. "Let's get out of here."

As they walked up the road, she said, "They said you've been in jail before."

He slowly nodded, and she pulled on his arm.

"Tell me about it?"

"I need to eat." He nodded his head to a nearby diner. "It's quite a long story."

As they sat and ate steak sandwiches and fries, Benjamin began, "You remember how I told you about Kylie and driving her home?" Pattie's eyes grew wide and she nodded. "When I got there her ex-boyfriend was there, like I told you, but what I didn't tell you was that when he left, he drove to a police station and told them I'd punched him. Then he got me arrested for assault. I didn't have the money for bail and I just couldn't ask my folks. I was staying at my cousin's at the time and he had no money, so I sat in jail for a whole year. Eventually, the charges must've been dropped because they let me out."

"That's awful."

"I know. Kylie kept writing to me. Sometimes, she'd write five or six times a week. I answered a couple of the letters until I realized she was developing a fixation on me. And, you know the rest."

"Why didn't you tell me all this?"

"I was embarrassed, and I didn't want *Mamm* to find out. She'd take things to heart and she's all about reputation, and she's only just gotten over the shame of Timothy and Taylor and them ... well, you know what happened."

*"Jah,* she was an *Englischer,* and Taylor got pregnant while Timothy was on his *rumspringa."*

Benjamin nodded. It wasn't a secret. Everyone in the whole community knew it. "Now, they are happily married with three *kinner."* He leaned forward and stared into her big brown eyes. "Now it's your turn."

"My turn for what?"

"What's the story with this Stephen guy?"

"Oh, that. He's an *Englischer* I dated a while ago. I met him at work."

"Oh, wonderful choice." He popped a fry into his mouth.

"At least he admitted he did it. He told the police it was just meant to scare me." She shook her head. "I made a terrible mistake going out with him."

"Now I don't feel so bad." He chuckled, figuring she couldn't be mad at him for driving an *Englisch* girl home in broad daylight if she had agreed to go on a date with an *Englischer.* "We've both made bad choices."

"Hey, I didn't say I was marrying the guy."

He chuckled again. "Still, you can't be so hard on me now. And Kylie's the one who made up the engagement story."

"I suppose I can forgive you just a little for keeping so many secrets."

"Hey, it was just one." He leaned closer. "How much will you forgive me?"

She held up her hand and pinched her fingers together so they were an inch apart. "About this much."

"I'll take it. You've got to admit we make a good pair."

She shook her head and giggled. "I think you should tell your *mudder* what you just told me about being in jail."

"I don't want to talk about her right now. I want to talk about us."

Her cheeks turned crimson. "What about us?"

"Like I said, we make a good pair and I think we should become official."

"A real couple?"

*"Jah."*

"We haven't even been on a proper date."

He looked around. "This is a date."

*"Nee,* this is just talking somewhere."

"I'll collect you for a buggy ride tomorrow. How's that?"

She giggled. "Okay."

# CHAPTER 24

WHEN THEY GOT BACK to his house no one was home. "I've got no idea where they are. *Mamm's* usually home at this time of day," Benjamin said.

"It's cold, let's go inside." Once they were sitting by the fire, Pattie said, "I think Stephen confessed when they told him they had his fingerprints. He only meant to frighten me."

"He did a good job of that."

"Hmm. That's true. I hope I don't ever have to see Stephen again."

"We could introduce him to Kylie."

They both laughed.

Pattie said, "I guess I could forgive you for all the dreadful things you've done if you make me a cup of *kaffe.*"

"The things I've done?"

*"Jah."*

"I've still got the snow to finish clearing away from your door. You seem to have had a lot more snow at your place than we've had here."

"It'll melt in time. Now, how about that *kaffe?*"

He rolled his eyes. "On one condition."

"What's that?"

"You come into the kitchen and talk to me while I make it."

"Okay. I can do that."

"If you're nice, I can even make you something to eat," Benjamin said.

"You can cook?"

"Of course. Pretty well, too. I've been mostly looking after myself these past few years. I can even patch my own clothes if I have to."

They both jumped up and looked out the window when they heard a buggy.

"Here they are. You must tell them everything."

Benjamin gulped. "You think?"

*"Jah.* I'll stay in my room. Tell them I'm lying down and then tell them what happened."

Benjamin nodded and Pattie went up the stairs after touching him reassuringly on his arm.

BENJAMIN WASN'T LOOKING FORWARD to telling his parents about being in jail for nearly a year. It had been because of a false accusation, but that wouldn't matter to the rumormongers. He could imagine his mother crying and running out of the room — *'the shame, the shame of it all,' she'd cry. 'First Timothy and now Benjamin. Our lives are ruined.'*

He shook his head. Perhaps his father would be more understanding? He had given Pattie his word that he would tell them, and perhaps it was better that way. It would be much worse if they found out from someone else. Particularly someone in the community.

He opened the door just as his mother stepped onto the porch.

"Why did the police arrest you?"

"I'll wait until *Dat* comes inside and I'll tell you both together."

WHEN BOTH HIS parents were sitting down in the living room, his father on the armchair and his mother on the couch, he sat down next to his mother. They were strangely silent. Maybe they had found out already somehow.

He cleared his throat. "The good news is that they found the person who burned down the Rieds' house."

"Who was it?" his mother asked.

"Just some young man. No one from the Amish. Probably did it for kicks. The police chased him and found him through his fingerprints."

"And what did the police want with you?" his father asked him.

"Well, that's quite a long story." He closed his eyes to

say a silent prayer and when he opened them he saw his parents' eyes glued to him. "I was in jail for a year," he blurted out. His father's eyebrows rose, and his mother's jaw dropped open.

"What do you mean?" she asked him.

"Someone accused me of something I didn't do. A man was trying to fight me and he tripped and fell when I ducked out of the way of his punch, and he knocked his head on my buggy. He told the police I did it, that I'd hit him. Long story short, I got thrown in jail. I didn't want to ask you for bail money, so I sat and roasted in jail for several months."

"Why didn't you tell us?" Mr. Fuller asked.

"I didn't want to worry you."

"We would've given you bail money," Mr. Fuller said.

"I didn't want either of you to know. I would've been the only son out of seven to be in jail. That would've upset you, wouldn't it, *Mamm?*"

"Not if you were innocent."

"Well, I was."

"Exactly when were you in jail?" his father asked.

"It was a long time ago now. I can't tell you the details because I had someone cover for me."

"No good ever comes of covering up a lie," Mr. Fuller said.

"I know that. I know I should've said something, but I didn't want to upset anyone, so I thought it would be better just to keep quiet about the whole thing."

Mrs. Fuller put her hand to her cheek. "Was it terrible in jail?"

"The food was dreadful, tasteless, but I made some good friends in there." From the look on her face, it was clear that his mother didn't like the sound of that. "They're just people, *Mamm.* People like you and me. Some of them have been wrongly accused as well, and others made mistakes. They're just regular folk, most of them."

"I'm glad you finally told us," Mrs. Fuller said.

Benjamin sighed. "If I'd known you were going to take it this well I'd have asked you for the bail money."

"How did you get out?" Mr. Fuller asked.

"The charges were dropped all of a sudden. Maybe there was no proof or the guy didn't want to testify in court. I'm not sure. No one ever told me."

His father raised his hand. "Now wait a minute. How is it that you could volunteer as a firefighter with a record?"

"Technically, I don't have a record because the charges were dropped, so there was no problem. They had my prints in the system because I'd been in jail. Besides, that, I joined the firefighters prior to needing the criminal history checks done."

"Ah."

## CHAPTER 25

Later that night, at their middle-of-the-night chamomile-tea rendezvous, Benjamin thanked Pattie for encouraging him to talk with his parents.

"I told you it would go well. You should listen to me more often. Now, drink your tea or it will go cold."

He chuckled and looked into her brown eyes. There was something about this young woman that captivated him like no other had done. "Marry me, Pattie."

"Okay." She took a sip of her tea.

"Did you hear me?"

*"Jah."*

He frowned at her. This was too easy; she had to be teasing him. "I asked you to marry me."

"I said I would."

"As easy as that?"

"Do you want it to be more difficult?" Her brown eyes sparkled with mischief and left him speechless.

She leaned over and kissed his cheek and sent his heart racing.

He laughed and took hold of her hand. With a woman like Pattie, he'd never be bored. Had she resisted him all along to be playful, appearing to be uninterested? It didn't matter, there was something about her that made him want to keep her close and protect her from harm forever. "You're serious, you will marry me? I don't have to prove myself? There's no waiting for this or for that?"

"We don't have to wait for anything. Although, an autumn wedding would be nice."

"An autumn wedding it is. And, I'm going to go back to work in the family business."

"If that makes you happy then do it."

He nodded. "I think it will. Now, that you've come to your senses about me, I think it will."

When Pattie giggled, it was sweet music to Benjamin's ears.

EVEN THOUGH HER house was completed months ago, Pattie stayed the night before her wedding at the Fullers' home, where Ivy had volunteered to host the ceremony and the meal. Pattie had gotten no sleep because she was so excited to be married and have her own family at last. That was something she'd craved ever since she'd lost her parents. A husband and *kinner* would surely help fill the void in her heart.

It was dawn when she tiptoed into the kitchen to make herself a cup of strong coffee. She didn't expect there would be anyone else awake, but Mrs. Fuller sat at the table crying into a handkerchief.

Pattie rushed toward her and put her arm around the woman's shoulder. "Ivy, is something wrong?"

Startled, Ivy dropped the handkerchief and looked at her. *"Nee.* Nothing's wrong."

Pattie sat down opposite her. "Then why the tears?"

"My last son is getting married. You see, I had seven and now, in a little while, I will have none."

Pattie blinked back tears of her own. She always cried when she saw someone else crying. "You won't be losing him. We'll be living in my *haus* and that's not too far."

"He won't listen to me anymore. He'll listen to you."

Pattie giggled. "Did he ever listen to you?"

Ivy smiled. "Not lately."

"You see? He'll just keep being Benjamin, and keep doing his own thing like he's always done. I don't think he'll ever listen to anyone. Although, he might've when he was younger."

Mrs. Fuller dabbed at her eyes. "I'm being silly."

"You'll still be needed."

"I haven't been needed for a long time."

"Ivy, you're the glue that holds this family together.

You're the pastry crust around the apple pie, the cream in the whoopie pies."

Ivy chuckled.

"Everyone looks to you for guidance, and everyone respects you and Obadiah. You're done a great job in raising seven *wunderbaar* sons. Can you teach me what to do when my time comes? I've got no idea how to raise *kinner,* and I have no *mudder* of my own to guide me."

Ivy blinked rapidly. "Being a *mudder* is instinct."

"And practice, I'm sure, and I've had none of that. Don't cry, because you'll make me cry and I don't want to do that today."

A hint of a smile met Ivy's lips. "Why are you awake so early?"

Pattie looked out the window at the first beams of morning sun trying to peep over the horizon. "I couldn't sleep. Today, a brand-new chapter of my life begins. I never thought I'd get married so young, but it happened."

"I think *Gott* likes to surprise us sometimes."

"I've had my share of those. I don't mind the good ones, but I don't like the bad."

"And you've had enough of those." Ivy grabbed hold of Pattie's hand. "Allow me and Obadiah to be your replacement *mudder* and *vadder.*"

"That's what you'll be today, officially." Pattie smiled at her soon-to-be mother-in-law. "Of all the *mudders*-

in-law I could've had, I'm glad you're Benjamin's *Mamm.*"

"We gladly welcome you into our *familye.*"

PATTIE BLINKED back tears when she stood beside Benjamin in front of the bishop. She wore a midnight-blue dress, and a matched set of sheer white organza *kapp,* apron and cape, all lovingly made for her by Mary Lou. All the while, Pattie was counting her blessings. She was no longer alone. Not only did she have the love of her life, Benjamin, she had a slew of brothers-in-law and sisters-in-law, not to mention all of the nieces and nephews. She still missed her parents dearly, but her heart had mended and she deeply appreciated Ivy and Obadiah offering to assume the role of parents to her rather than just parents-in-law. She glanced up at her tall handsome husband, her protector, in his dark suit and bowtie and couldn't imagine a life without him at the center.

BENJAMIN FELT Pattie looking at him and he glanced at her and they exchanged a quick smile before they looked back to the front. She was the most beautiful and intriguing young woman he'd ever met. He thanked God that their paths crossed when they did, although he was sad it had taken misfortune to make it happen. Her house fire had caused her to stay with his parents, and had he not volunteered as a firefighter, he might never have gotten together with her, especially considering she was so much younger than he.

He had often thought about love in recent years, and what it would be like to find 'the one.' The only way he could describe it was that Pattie and he fitted together like two compatibly-misshapen pieces of a large jig-saw puzzle. He'd found the missing part of himself, and each of them completed the other.

~

PATTIE AND BENJAMIN'S wedding was the next time Magnolia saw Zach. Amish weddings were normally held at the bride's parents' house, but Pattie was orphaned and thus it was being held at the Fullers' house. Now Zach and Pattie's rebuilt house was to be Benjamin and Pattie's place, at least until Benjamin built them their own home. They'd also discussed buying out Zach's share of the restored *haus,* but Zach had told them there was no hurry to decide.

Zach made his way over to Magnolia when she was by herself. "Can we talk?" he asked meekly.

She nodded and hoped he didn't think they could forget things and move on.

He suggested, "Can we go by the barn? It's quieter there."

She agreed and followed him along a row of trees and then behind the barn. The trees towering nearby had changed to shades of orange and brown, and a golden carpet of leaves lay under their feet.

He turned around to face her.

"Allow me to start." Magnolia cleared her throat. "I did some dreadful things. I was miserable and wretched and just wanted someone to share my life with. Nothing I did turned out right. So, I've given up. All of my students are my *kinner* now, and that's all the love I need in my life. I'm boarding with the Wallaces and have a lovely room overlooking the countryside. What more could I want?"

"I'll tell you."

*"Nee.* I don't want anything else!" Magnolia turned and walked away. She guessed that he liked her, but probably only because she was no longer interested. She'd had to harden her heart against romantic love. It was something that was never going to happen, not for her.

He grabbed her arm and swung her around to face him. "Marry me, Magnolia?"

She was shocked at his words, and even more shocked at the way he'd man-handled her. "I'll do no such thing." She stared at his hand on her arm. "Let me go."

"Never. I let you go once and I'll never let you go again."

"Stop it or I'll ... I'll ... scream."

He moved closer to her instead, and pulled her into his arms. She felt helpless and could no longer resist him. His hand went around her waist and now her body was pulled in against his. Her heart thumped hard as he lowered his mouth against hers. Closing her eyes, she savored the masculine scent of his body and the touch of his warm lips. Then she stopped herself. She didn't deserve happiness, and she pushed herself away from him. *"Nee!* Stop it, Zach." Things had been ruined between them many months ago.

"I won't. I can't lose you, Magnolia."

"You can't lose what you've never had." She turned and made to walk away, but he jumped in front of her. "Look, Zach, I'm flattered, in a way, but you don't know the real me. I'm … I've done some things that a nice person wouldn't do."

"I'm sure we've all done some things we're not proud of."

She raised her eyebrows. "What have you done?"

"Many awful things. One of which was believing that awful rumor." He looked down and shook his head. "If I told you more, you'd hate me."

She frowned. "Stop making fun of me."

He stepped closer and took hold of her hands. "Magnolia, we got along so well before I thought you burned down my *haus.* I've never been able to talk to a girl the way I talked to you. And even though we probably only spent a day or two together if you add up all the hours, everything feels so natural with you and so right. Won't you forgive me for listening to gossip?"

"You should've known I'd never do anything so

horrible. I can forgive, but I don't think I could ever forget."

"People told me some things you'd done and I built things up in my mind and thought you might have done the other thing as well. Can you find forgiveness in your heart?"

"Maybe I can one day. I can't marry you, though. Miss Shwetz never married."

"That's because no one ever asked Miss Shwetz."

Magnolia gasped. "You know her?"

*"Nee,* but I've known plenty of old women who never married and you're nothing like them."

"I'm not?"

*"Nee,* I've seen you with Mary Lou's *kinner.* You're so gentle and patient. That tells me what a good person you are. I knew it right away anyway, as soon as I met you. There's no better woman for me in the whole world. I want you to be the *mudder* of my *kinner.* We'll tell our *grosskinner* a funny story of how I thought you burned the *haus* to the ground to make me come home so I could meet you."

Magnolia pulled a face. "It'll take me that long before I could possibly find it funny."

"Is that a yes?"

*"Nee."*

"Will you think about it at least?"

Magnolia licked her lips. She didn't want to upset him. "What we had has been ruined, and it's been ruined not by me, but by you. I can't feel the same about you because you thought I did that dreadful thing. I can't forget you thought I was capable of doing something so dreadful." She shook her head and groaned. "Do you see?"

His face fell, his lips downturned and he slowly released her hands. She walked away from him and never looked back.

Magnolia remembered the night of the fire at Pattie's house; something had always weighed on her mind since then. She rushed to find Mary Lou. It was fortunate to see her without her *kinner,* talking to Lucy.

"Excuse me, Lucy. Might I have a quick word with you alone, Mary Lou?"

"*Jah,* of course."

The two walked a little away from the crowd, and Magnolia swallowed hard. "That night of the fire, back when Pattie and Zach's *haus* burned down. I was out walking and I saw the glow reflected in the clouds of the night sky."

"You were out alone at night—that night?"

"I wanted to talk to *Gott* and I do that best alone and outdoors."

"Go on," Mary Lou said.

"Don't you see? Do I have to spell it out?" When Mary Lou nodded with a vacant look on her face, Magnolia said, "I knew it was a fire, most likely, and I did nothing. I didn't think it would've been a *haus,* but still, I did nothing. *Gott* can't be happy. I confessed to Him, but I think He wants me to tell someone,

someone like you." She stared in her cousin's face hoping she'd say it wasn't a big deal.

Mary Lou smiled and looped her arm through her cousin's. "That was a long time ago, Magnolia, and you weren't to know what it was."

Magnolia nodded. "You don't think I'm a bad person?"

"*Nee,* not at all. I saw your boots by the door that night."

"You knew I'd seen the fire?"

Mary Lou shook her head. "I didn't, but I knew that you'd been out walking that night."

"You never said anything."

"I knew … well, I thought you might say something if you'd seen it. A fire is often seen at night by the glow in the sky if nothing else."

"I feel so much better for saying something. I don't know why I kept quiet at the time. I was such a wretched person back then, only caring about myself and my problems. Being a teacher has changed my life."

"*Gut.* I'm glad to hear it. You seem so much happier these days."

Magnolia smiled and felt as though things had come full circle. In a way, it had felt good to turn Zach down. Now she was in control of her life. She didn't need to wait for a man to propose. Did she need a man at all? No, she decided she didn't, and that was a good feeling.

ZACH SOON RETURNED to Chester County and resumed working with his friend in the racehorse and buggy business.

IT WAS two years later before Magnolia felt ready to love again. She'd forgiven herself for the things she'd done in the past and had sought forgiveness from the people she'd wronged. The idea of living life as Miss Shwetz had flown right out the window the moment Magnolia laid eyes on Caleb Smith. He was a widower and the father of one of her new students. He was a distant cousin of the Miller girls; the ones who'd married three of the Fuller boys. Six months after his wife's death, Caleb had decided to move here with his young son to make a fresh start, taking a job working for the Fullers. With Caleb, Magnolia found there was no need for scheming, or plotting. From the moment they met, the two of them got along like they'd always known one another. They married within six months of meeting and a year later welcomed a baby girl into their family. Magnolia had what she'd always wanted. If she'd settled for Zach, she would've missed out on so much more.

TWO WEEKS after hearing the news that Magnolia had married, Zach proposed to a girl from Galveston whose father owned a horse ranch, and a hasty marriage was entered into.

*The Fullers*

IVY AND OBADIAH FULLER relaxed in their golden years knowing their seven sons had married good women and were living within the faith with happy marriages and families. Each son had taken his own sweet time finding love, but once they had found it, they knew it was right. With the number of their grandchildren rapidly increasing, the cycle of life continued for another generation of the Fullers.

~

AMISH BACHELOR'S SECRET is Book 7 and the final in the *Seven Amish Bachelors* series.

I do hope you enjoyed the books.

Samantha Price.

~

## SEVEN AMISH BACHELORS

Book 1 The Amish Bachelor

Book 2 His Amish Romance

Book 3 Joshua's Choice

Book 4 Forbidden Amish Romance

Book 5 The Quiet Amish Bachelor

Book 6 The Determined Amish Bachelor

Book 7 Amish Bachelor's Secret

## OTHER BOOKS BY SAMANTHA PRICE:

Stand-Alone Christmas novel:

In Time For An Amish Christmas

Book series:

EXPECTANT AMISH WIDOWS

Book 1 Amish Widow's Hope

Book 2 The Pregnant Amish Widow

Book 3 Amish Widow's Faith

Book 4 Their Son's Amish Baby

Book 5 Amish Widow's Proposal

Book 6 The Pregnant Amish Nanny

Book 7 A Pregnant Widow's Amish Vacation

Book 8 The Amish Firefighter's Widow

Book 9 Amish Widow's Secret

Book 10 The Middle-Aged Amish Widow

Book 11 Amish Widow's Escape

Book 12 Amish Widow's Christmas

Book 13 Amish Widow's New Hope

Book 14 Amish Widow's Story

Book 15 Amish Widow's Decision

Book 16 Amish Widow's Trust

AMISH MISFITS

Book 1 The Amish Girl Who Never Belonged

Book 2 The Amish Spinster

BOOK 3 The Amish Bishop's Daughter

Book 4 The Amish Single Mother

Book 5 The Temporary Amish Nanny

Book 6 Jeremiah's Daughter

AMISH LOVE BLOOMS

Book 1 Amish Rose

Book 2 Amish Tulip

Book 3 Amish Daisy

Book 4 Amish Lily

Book 5 Amish Violet

Book 6 Amish Willow

AMISH BRIDES

Book 1 Arranged Marriage

Book 2 Falling in Love

Book 3 Finding Love

Book 4 Amish Second Loves

Book 5 Amish Silence

AMISH TWIN HEARTS

Book 1 Amish Trading Places

Book 2 Amish Truth Be Told

Book 3 The Big Beautiful Amish Woman

Book 4 The Amish Widow and the Millionaire

AMISH ROMANCE SECRETS

Book 1 A Simple Choice

Book 2 Annie's Faith

Book 3 A Small Secret

Book 4 Ephraim's Chance

Book 5 A Second Chance

Book 6 Choosing Amish

AMISH WEDDING SEASON

Book 1 Impossible Love

Book 2 Love at First

Book 3 Faith's Love

Book 4 The Trials of Mrs. Fisher

Book 5 A Simple Change

AMISH SECRET WIDOWS' SOCIETY (Cozy Mystery Series)

Book 1 The Amish Widow

Book 2 Hidden

Book 3 Accused

Book 4 Amish Regrets

Book 5 Amish House of Secrets

Book 6 Amish Undercover

Book 7 Amish Breaking Point

Book 8 Plain Murder

Book 9 Plain Wrong

Book 10 Amish Mystery: That Which Was Lost

# ABOUT THE AUTHOR

Samantha Price is a best selling author who knew she wanted to become a writer at the age of seven, while her grandmother read to her Peter Rabbit in the sun room. Though the adventures of Peter and his sisters Flopsy, Mopsy, and Cotton-tail started Samantha on her creative journey, it is now her love of Amish culture that inspires her to write. Her writing is clean and wholesome, with more than a dash of sweetness. Though she has penned over eighty Amish Romance and Amish Mystery books, Samantha is just as in love today with exploring the spiritual and emotional journeys of her characters as she was the day she first put pen to paper. Samantha lives in a quaint Victorian cottage with three rambunctious dogs.

www.samanthapriceauthor.com
samanthaprice333@gmail.com
www.facebook.com/SamanthaPriceAuthor
Follow Samantha Price on BookBub
Twitter @ AmishRomance

Made in the USA
Lexington, KY
06 August 2018